GREATEST HITS
A SHORT STORY COLLECTION
By
T. M. Bilderback

I0549629

This collection, Greatest Hits, is ©2014 by T. M. Bilderback

Other Works By T. M. Bilderback

SOMEONE SAVED MY LIFE TONIGHT

A JUSTICE SECURITY SHORT STORY

G us Brazzle felt very spiffy in his uniform. His badge gleamed in the early morning sunlight that shone through the bedroom window. There wasn't a speck of lint to be found on the sharply creased slacks or the slightly starched, over-ironed shirt. The collar button on Gus's shirt was open, and his shoes were so polished, he could see himself in them.

He reached for his nightstick and added it to the special loop on his belt. His radio, the lifeline to backup, was also clipped to his belt. The holster that held his Glock semiautomatic pistol remained on his dresser. His assignment didn't require him to go armed.

The gleaming badge read, "Justice Security" at the top. Underneath that, in smaller letters, appeared the words, "Uniform Security Division." And, below that phrase, was "Brazzle – 759."

Gus worked for Justice Security's uniformed security division. The head person in the uniformed division, or Gus's boss, was Tony Armstrong. Tony manned the main desk at Justice Security, and watched over the company's comings and goings...but, he also oversaw the "grunts," as they were called by the plainclothes security personnel. The partners that were responsible for forming and maintaining the security company also divided up the responsibilities of various divisions. The partner ultimately in charge of the "grunts" was Misty Wilhite, founding partner of the company, and longtime girlfriend of Joey Justice, after whom the company had been named.

Gus liked Misty very much.

Gus had never married. The right woman had never crossed his path. As a result, he had no children...that he knew of, of course. He chuckled to himself at that old joke. But, Misty was like the daughter he never had...and he was quite determined to never give her a reason to be less than proud of him, both as a person and an employee.

Gus's current assignment was security at a used book, movie, and music store. Misty was going to make an appearance at the store to observe and inspect Gus, and talk with the clients. Gus wasn't worried about any of it, since the clients would have nothing but good things to say.

Gus had retired from the Army at forty, after he had done his twenty years. He had been a Master Sergeant for the final five years. His military pension was more than enough to live on, but Gus felt lost spending his days doing nothing. He had tried working security for a few other companies before he finally came to Justice Security. He had been very happy with them, and had been with them for a few years. Now, at age sixty-seven, he was giving serious consideration to finally retiring permanently.

One more quick look in the mirror, and he gave himself his own approval. Snapping a quick salute to himself, he placed the envelope containing his will in plain sight on the dresser, propped against the mirror. It was an old habit, and probably would never be necessary...but it helped to be prepared. He left his bedroom and his house, and climbed into his car for the drive to the bookstore.

As he drove the city's streets, he remembered another reason to enjoy the day today. It was Tuesday...and that meant that he could spend time with Nicole.

If Misty Wilhite was the daughter Gus had never had, Nicole was the granddaughter he had never had. Nicole was five years old, and the daughter of one of the bookstore's clerks. The clerk, Teresa Ambrose, was a single mother and a college student. She had grants and student loans to help with her education, along with child support. It wasn't enough. Teresa worked part-time at the bookstore on Tuesdays and Thursdays to help make ends meet. She could not afford child care, so she brought Nicole to work.

Nicole was a very well-behaved little girl, and was much loved by everyone at the bookstore. However, she had developed a strong attachment to Gus. Because of his brown uniform, she had nicknamed him "Sugar Bear." They played "Hide and Seek" among the shelves, and Nicole would giggle every time that Gus found her. From his primary post beside the exit door, Gus would read to her, often for several hours a day.

Teresa had asked Gus to come to dinner several times, and he had accepted. He also had invited Teresa and Nicole over to his house as well. He often performed babysitting duties for Teresa, and had given her occasional help by paying her rent or her electric bill if her money was particularly short that month. On the times he had done this, he made certain that Teresa knew that it was done for love of Nicole, and that there were no strings attached whatsoever. He absolutely adored the child.

It was going to be a great day.

Brian Curtis awoke from a nightmare. This was nothing unusual in Brian's world – nightmares were the only dreams he ever remembered.

Wide awake and covered with sweat, Brian sat on the side of his squalid bed. He moved the cheap bedsheet curtain to one side of the window, and stared blankly at his view of Hooker Hollow, otherwise known as Fourth Street in this city. He could hear sirens approaching in the distance, screaming their way to the latest robbery...or the latest assault...or the latest overdose...or the latest murder. It didn't matter much which piece of crime applied – the sirens were always present, and always the same. No one paid attention to them anymore.

Brian's head didn't hurt. At least, it didn't hurt from a hangover. He had spent some time in McFeely's Bar (known on the street as "McFeelme's") last night, but he had only had a couple of beers. He had been far too angry to get drunk. He had taken some perfectly fine books and DVDs to the used bookstore, hoping to gain a bit of cash to feed himself. The bookstore had refused to buy any of them, and had asked Brian not to return to the store. The old security guard had asked him to leave the store immediately, and had put his hand on his nightstick. Brian had gotten the hint...but had made sure that he expressed his feelings at his mistreatment. He expressed them quite colorfully, and at extreme volume.

His head *did* hurt, however. The voices wouldn't shut up this morning. And they were telling him exactly what to do to get even with that bookstore.

Gus's shift at the bookstore was noon until eight each night. He pulled into the parking lot at exactly eleven-fifty. Clocking in was a simple radio call to his boss, Tony Armstrong, who logged Gus as being onsite at the bookstore.

"Hey, Gus-gus," said Tony, over the radio. "The misty-ress will be in the house at approximately two this afternoon. Please let the bread-and-butter people know. Copy?"

Gus smiled. Tony was telling him to expect Misty Wilhite at two that afternoon, and to inform the clients of that fact. He keyed the radio. "Roger that, Tony. We'll have a nice conversation. You take care, now, and have a good day. Copy?"

"Copy. You do the same, Sergeant."

Gus smiled again and clipped his radio back into place on his belt. He then got out of his car and headed inside the bookstore. As he walked through the front door, a three-foot-two torpedo barreled into his legs.

"Sugar Bear!" shouted Nicole as she hugged Gus's legs.

Gus reached down and scooped the girl up into his arms. "Hi, Nicki-poo." He tickled her under her chin. She giggled and ducked her head down, clasping her hands to her throat. "You been a good girl?"

Nicole nodded while she said, "Yep."

Gus looked at her face thoughtfully. "Hmmm...I don't know about that. I think I see a little meanness leaking out of your ear..." He reached up to her ear, touched it quickly with the tip of his finger, then pulled his hand away from it. Gus opened his hand to show a shiny new quarter. "Well. Guess I was wrong. It was only a quarter."

"Can I have it, Sugar Bear?" asked Nicole.

"Don't see why not. It came out of *your* ear, didn't it?" He gave her the quarter and set her down on the floor. "Now, what are you going to do with it, little one?"

"Put it in my pig with the others," she replied. She turned and ran behind the counter to her mother. "Mommy! Will you put this quarter in your pocket? We have to put it in my pig later!"

Teresa smiled at her daughter. "You bet, Nickie-chick!" She took the quarter and put it into her jeans pocket. "There we go. Now, let's not forget it, okay?"

"Okay, Mommy."

Teresa looked up at Gus and smiled. "Hi, Gus. What's happening?"

"Not much, Terry-girl," said Gus. "Misty's coming by later to talk to the clients and to make sure that I'm doing what I'm supposed to be doing. Did you hear about the guy yesterday?"

Teresa shook her head. "No, what happened?"

Gus shook his head. "I really thought for a minute that I was going to have to use my stick on him. He came in with some old, stained paperback books and a couple of scratched movies. He was filthy, Teresa, and the smell? Oh, boy...I smelled latrines in the service that smelled better! He was mumbling to himself the whole time he was here, and when Chapman told him that he couldn't use what the guy had, the guy started talking dirty, threatening to hurt him if he didn't give him some money for the stuff. Chapman told him that his stuff was trash, and told him to leave the store and never come back. I had stepped over, and when Chapman told the guy that, the guy started cursing at the top of his lungs, waving his arms all around...wow. I had to put my hand on his elbow, and I hated to do it, but I had to get him out of the store. There were kids in here, and he was scaring them." Gus shook his head in disgust. "I bet I washed my hands for ten minutes. Very few people scare me, but that guy did."

The guy in question was at that moment driving a stolen service truck full of tools and ladders. Brian had "borrowed" the truck after a discussion with the truck's owner. The truck owner strongly disagreed with loaning the truck and its contents to Brian, but gave up his argument after Brian showed the owner a new and special way to use a large pipe wrench. The owner offered no argument when Brian borrowed the coveralls the owner was wearing. The bloodstains were minute, and could easily be dismissed as grease, paint, or other legitimate work stains. Brian had left the owner inside a dumpster, and hoped that the owner's family would display the man in a manner that showed off the new shape of the owner's head after the special application of the pipe wrench.

Brian had arrived at the bookstore, and had parked in the alley in back. The building was only two stories high, so Brian took the extension ladder from its hooks and extended it to the flat roof of the building. He guessed that he would need to make several trips to carry his ingredients to the roof, but that it wouldn't be too difficult.

One of the voices in his head told him that he should stop what he was doing and run. He pulled the brim of the baseball hat he was wearing down, stifled the voice, and started climbing and carrying.

Gus took his post. Sometimes he would stand, and sometimes he would sit on a tall, kitchen-type stool. When Nicole brought books for him to read to her, he would sit on the stool and pull her up onto his knee.

Business was steady, which was typical for a Tuesday. Mostly the store had college students and housewives for customers in the middle of the week, which meant that Gus could spend time playing and reading.

At two o'clock, Misty Wilhite came into the store, looking friendly and beautiful, as always. She came over to Gus and gave him a big hug.

"Hi, Gus!" she said. "How's tricks?"

Gus was smiling. "Tricks are nothing but treats in disguise, Misty. All is quiet on the reading front."

Misty smiled. "So glad to hear it, Gus." She gestured to the spot on his belt where his holster would normally be. "You sure about not going armed? You're sort of close to some dangerous spots here."

Gus shook his head. "No. I saw enough shootings in the war. I'll carry it if I'm ordered to, or if the assignment requires it. Other than that, I have the old 'persuader' here." He put his hand on the handle of his nightstick.

Misty nodded. "Your call, Gus. Just be careful. Please." She caught a glimpse of a small head peeking out at her from behind Gus's stool. "Also, Gus, can you tell me if that little Nicole is still a rotten..." She had hunched down, and put out her hands on either side of her body, much like a wrestler. "...spoiled..." She took a couple of fake menacing steps toward Nicole, who had started giggling nervously. "...little brat?" And, with the word "brat," Misty had grabbed Nicole and started tickling her. Both Misty and Nicole were laughing and wrestling around, while Gus watched with a huge grin on his face.

After a moment, Misty gave Nicole a big hug and set her on her feet. "So, tell me, Miss Nicole-the-brat, is anyone manning the front desk today?"

Nicole said, "Yep, my mommy."

"Would you take me to her?"

"Okay. And I'm not a brat!" Nicole ran to the front desk, giggling.

Misty looked up at Gus. "Guess us two brats will get out of your hair, Gus. Need anything?"

"Everything is fine, Misty."

Misty nodded and headed for the front desk. Teresa was waiting for her, with Nicole sitting on another stool beside her.

"Hi, Teresa," said Misty. "Is Chapman here today?"

"Hello, Misty. Yeah, he's upstairs. Come on, I'll take you." She came out from behind the counter, held her hand out to Nicole, and said, "Take Mommy's hand, baby." Then, louder, "Gus! We're going upstairs for a minute! Can you watch the front counter?"

Gus waved and acknowledged that he would.

The ladies walked to the back of the store, entered the back storeroom, and began climbing the stairs. They chatted inconsequentially as they climbed. At the top of the stairs, the smell of fresh paint hit them.

"Oh, wow, stinky," said Teresa, and put her hand over her nose and mouth. To Nicole she said, "Baby, go downstairs to Gus and wait for me, okay?"

Nicole nodded and ran down the stairs.

Teresa and Misty walked down the office corridor to an open storage room filled with filing cabinets and merchandise. On one wall, a man in paint-stained coveralls was using a roller to apply fresh, white paint to the walls. Plastic sheeting used as drop cloths were spread over everything in the room.

"Oh, hi," said Teresa to the painter. "Can you tell me if Chapman is up here?"

The painter turned toward the ladies. "He left just a few minutes ago. He said something about going to get something to eat."

Teresa looked at Misty, puzzled. "That's weird...he didn't say anything to me, and I didn't see him leave."

The man shrugged. "I dunno, lady. All I know is that I gotta finish this job and be outta here by five." He started painting again.

Teresa again looked at Misty. "I'm so sorry, Misty. He knew you would be here today. Maybe he just forgot the time."

Misty smiled and shook her head. "No problem, Teresa. I'll just catch him another day. Let me go tickle Nicole a bit more, and say goodbye to Gus, and I'll be on my way."

They went downstairs, leaving the painter to finish his work.

Brian breathed a small sigh of relief after the women went back downstairs. Luckily, neither of them had seen him before, so he felt confident that he was in no danger.

The girl that talked to him obviously worked here, but Brian was more concerned with the other one. She looked familiar, like he had seen her on TV or something. He knew her...but he just couldn't place her. One of the voices asked him if it mattered who she was, and that if it would stop him if he remembered. Several of the other voices, including his own, said, "NO!" very firmly. Then, in the brief silence that followed, a small voice in his head asked if he thought he might have lost his mind. Several other voices again shouted out over the voice, and drowned it out.

He had been painting for about ten minutes. It had taken some time to add the proper amount of accelerant to each gallon of paint, mix it properly, then open the access door on the roof that led down some stairs to the second floor. He met the smart-alecky dude from yesterday, the one that the girl had called, "Chapman," and it was a toss-up which man was more surprised. Brian's reaction was faster, however: he punched Chapman in the solar plexus twice, then hit him on the head with a wooden mallet that was hanging from a loop on his coveralls. When Chapman hit the floor, Brian hit him twice more and looked around. He saw what he needed, retrieved it, and returned. Before Brian had disposed of him in the airshaft, Chapman had a DVD disc shoved into his mouth and a paperback novel rolled up and placed into another incorrect anatomical orifice.

Brian had to hurry, though...the festivities were going to start around seven.

The bookstore stayed open until seven-thirty on weeknights. At six forty-five, Gus was at his post, Teresa was behind the front counter, and Nicole was getting ready to play "Hide and Seek" with Gus.

Gus occasionally took a stroll through the store to show a security presence, and those were the times that he would "seek" Nicole. At six fifty-five, Gus went to the front counter and told Nicole to go hide.

"And you better hide really well, Nicki-poo, because this is the last time today! You've got five minutes, little one...so, go!"

And off the little girl ran, to hide as best she could somewhere in the store.

Brian had successfully painted all of the walls and ceilings on the second floor with his specially prepared paint, and had dribbled a trail up the stairs to the roof. The accelerant that he had added to the paint would burn whether the paint was dry or not.

All of the rollers, brushes, and paint cans were on the roof. Brian didn't plan on taking them with him, and they would add significant fuel.

The sun had just set on the city, and Brian checked his watch. Six fifty-five. Close enough. He struck a match, and, as he dropped it, two things happened simultaneously: First, he remembered that the lady he had seen earlier was Misty Wilhite, that she was a big mucky-muck with Justice Security, and that he had seen her on TV...on the news. Second, when the match hit the beginning of the paint trail, it fwoomped really big...and surprised Brian into taking a step backwards. He tripped over a paint roller, fell backwards, and shattered three of his neck vertebrae, which damaged his spinal cord, paralyzing him. He wasn't dead, but he couldn't move anything from the neck down.

Brian laughed like the crazy man he was, because the fires of hell were lit, and he was trapped, at night, at Ground Zero.

The fire, after its first initial birth, followed the paint trail down the stairs. Once down the roof stairs, the fire found a lot more fuel and tasted it. It liked the fuel very much, and began burning briskly. Within five minutes, the walls and ceilings were burning merrily, and the books and files had also began feeding the fire.

The second floor of the bookstore had become an inferno, and the fire greedily started looking for more fuel downstairs.

At seven, as Gus was about to start his walk through, one of the customers came to the front counter and said, "Hey, it smells like smoke in here."

Gus looked at Teresa and began walking toward the customer. As he did, he distinctly smelled the smoke.

Gus turned to Teresa and said, "Call the fire department, then go outside and wait. I'll round up the customers and send them out."

"Gus," said Teresa. "What about Nicole?"

Gus smiled at the worried mother. "Don't worry, Terri-girl. I'll find her and send her out, too. You just do what I said, okay?"

Teresa nodded and dialed the phone. Gus started rounding up customers. As he walked further into the store, he unclipped his radio and called it in.

"Badge 759 calling Justice Central. Please respond."

"Tony here, Gus-gus. What's wrong?"

"We've got a fire, Tony. Smells like a big one. I've got the counter girl calling the fire department, and I'm getting everyone out right now. Request backup, just in case."

"Roger that, Gus. You'll have backup on site within ten...fifteen at the latest. Be careful, my friend."

"Copy, Tony." Gus placed the radio back on his belt.

He spotted Nicole hiding on the bottom bookshelf midway into the store. He squatted down and looked into her face.

"Listen, Nicki-poo, and listen close," Gus said sternly. "I need you to go outside the front door and find your mother right now...do you understand me?"

Nicole nodded. "What's wrong, Gus?"

"Never you mind, Nicki. You just do what I told you. I have to look for any more customers. Now, go!" He swatted her behind to get her started and sent her running down the aisle.

After Nicole left, Gus walked through the store. All of the customers were out, thank God. He thought of Chapman...although he hadn't seen him today,

Teresa said that he was upstairs. Gus walked to the door of the back room and opened the door.

The back room was starting to burn, and was full of smoke. The stairs were burning fiercely, and there was no way Gus could make it up the stairs. If Chapman was up there, he was dead...poor guy.

Gus heard sirens in the distance, along with the horns that the big fire trucks used to blow through red lights. He started toward the front. Ten feet from the exit, the roof collapsed onto the floor of the second floor. Inside the store itself, a few pieces of ceiling between the support beams fell through, and the first floor was now on its way to becoming a flaming memory.

Gus ducked out the door.

Nicole had started toward the exit door, then remembered her blanket. It was behind the counter, so she ducked back behind it to retrieve her companion. While she was back there, she decided that she wanted her toys, and started gathering them up into her sleeping bag. As the child was doing this, the roof collapsed, and part of the ceiling fell through. The fire fell through with it, and scared Nicole into a corner behind the counter.

The first fire truck had arrived when Gus ducked out the exit door. It was parked about six feet from the door. As Gus came out, a fireman came up to him.

"Are you okay? Is there anyone else in there?"

"I'm fine, and everybody's out that I could find. There may or may not have been someone else on the second floor, but it's a moot point now, I guess."

The fireman nodded, and slapped Gus on the back. "Good job, man. We'll take it from here, then."

Gus nodded, and turned away. As he reached the back of the fire truck, Teresa ran up to him.

"Gus! Where's Nicole? Where is she?"

"I found her and sent her to the front! Didn't she come out?"

Teresa shook her head, then looked to the store. She burst into tears. The ground floor was burning almost out of control. The supports holding the ceiling couldn't last much longer.

Gus made his decision. He saw a fire-resistant fireman's coat on the back of the fire truck. He picked it up, put it on, and ran back into the store, ignoring the orders, shouted by the firemen, to stop.

The Channel Seven news van (The city's premier news team!) arrived just as Gus ducked inside the building. The cameraman, Steve, was also driving the van. His reporter partner, Miriam Apple, was riding shotgun.

"My God, Steve, did you see that?" Miriam said. "That security guard went back inside that building!"

Steve grunted, and climbed out of the van with his video camera. Miriam followed him, and told him to get shots of the burning bookstore. A fireman started jogging past her. Miriam grabbed his arm.

"Why did that guard go back inside?" she asked the fireman.

The fireman shook his head. "Word is that there's a kid inside."

Miriam looked at the building with wide eyes. "In there?" She thought to herself, There's no way anybody's still alive in that piece of hell!

Misty Wilhite had heard the radio conversation between Gus and Tony. She was at another client's facility, five minutes away from the bookstore. She excused herself, and drove quickly to the bookstore. She, too, arrived just in time to see Gus run back inside. She radioed back to Justice Security that backup would not be necessary, since she was on the scene.

"Does Gus have things under control, Misty?" asked Tony.

Misty thought for a moment before answering. "Tony, I believe he knows what he's doing. But it may be more than he can control." She put down the radio and went to find Teresa.

Inside the store, Gus looked around. The fire had rapidly overwhelmed the stacks of books. Shelves were burning, walls were burning, and smoke was everywhere. He could see the ceiling support beams were beginning to burn through – the roof was coming down very soon.

Gus couldn't guess which way to turn to look for Nicole, so he did something desperate. He yelled for her.

"Nicole! Where are you?"

Faintly, toward the counter, Gus heard, "Sugar Bear! Over here!"

Gus thought to himself, Oh, thank you, God! He ran to the front counter, counting on the coat to keep the fire from him. He skidded around the counter, and Nicole was there, crouched under the counter's shelf.

Nicole ran to him as soon as she saw him and jumped into his arms. "Oh, Sugar Bear, I knew you'd come get me!"

Gus hugged the child tightly. "Nicki-poo, coming back for you was the easy part. Getting us out of here is the problem now. We gotta go!"

Behind Gus, the support beams gave way. The ceiling collapsed between the counter and the exit door. They were cut off.

Miriam was looking around the gathered crowd, trying to find someone to interview, when she spotted Misty walking to Teresa. Steve the cameraman was still focused on the building.

Miriam quickly put some thoughts together. The fast glimpse she had of the guard...he had been wearing a brown uniform, just like Justice Security's uniformed division. Misty Wilhite was one of the founding partners of Justice Security. That meant this fire had something to do with Justice Security...and, in this city, Justice Security was news!

Miriam smacked Steve's arm and started toward Misty. Steve tagged along behind her.

"Miss Wilhite! Miss Wilhite!" shouted Miriam. Misty turned toward the ambitious reporter and winced. "What can you tell me about this fire? Is it related to any of the recent activities of Justice Security?"

Misty held up her hand to Miriam, with her palm toward the reporter's face. "Just a minute, Miriam, please?" Misty turned to Teresa. "What happened, and why did Gus duck back inside, Teresa?"

Teresa looked at Misty with haunted eyes. "Nicole's inside," she said in a low, toneless voice.

Just then, part of the ceiling collapsed inside the bookstore. Sparks flew out of broken windows, and flames immediately intensified with the rush of fresh oxygen.

Teresa fainted into Misty's arms.

Steve recorded it all.

Gus whirled around when the ceiling collapsed. He took in the situation in seconds.

Fire and debris stood between the exit door, which was the only remaining way out, and him and Nicole. In order to survive, they would have to cross twenty feet of burning debris.

They both would be severely burned, maybe killed by the fire. There was no way in the world that both of them could escape unhurt.

But, maybe...if he got a running start and hit the door with his shoulder...

Steve the cameraman had won Emmys for local news photography. He had won many other awards and accolades for his footage over the years. His instincts in a situation were always correct, and he always seemed to have the camera aimed where the action was.

Today was no exception.

While Misty was tending to Teresa, Miriam was haranguing Steve, yelling for him to record the futile attempts by the fire department to spray water on the fire. Steve, as usual, was ignoring the reporter and was focusing his camera on the exit door of the bookstore. He thought he had seen movement through his viewfinder.

He was right.

The exit door abruptly swung open.

What left the store was the stuff of nightmares.

It was Gus...or what was left of him. The skin on his face was a deep, lobster red in places, blackened in others. His eyes were shut, but it didn't matter – the heat had melted away his eyeballs. His ears were burned away to blackened stumps. His shirt, being partly polyester, had melted into his back, and his pants had almost burned away completely. His belt remained, and his nightstick was on fire.

Cradled in his arms was a small bundle, wrapped in the fireman's coat.

Miriam Apple, the hardened reporter, could only stare wordlessly at the apparition standing ten feet away from her. Misty quickly laid Teresa on the ground and ran to take the bundle from Gus. Parts of the skin of Gus's hands came away with the bundle. Gus tried to speak, but his vocal cords had been damaged from the heat, and his lungs were seared. He collapsed onto the ground, seeming to melt into the macadam of the parking lot. He was dead.

Misty gently laid the bundle on the ground and began unwrapping it, expecting the worst. As she opened the coat, she saw Nicole curled into a fetal position, holding her blanket, crying desperately. She wasn't hurt.

Gus had saved Nicole's life.

"In tonight's news, a fire at a downtown bookstore produced a hero. Here's Miriam Apple with the story."

"Tonight, a fire erupted at Chapman's Used Books downtown. Fire officials believe the fire was arson, and they think the arsonist perished in the fire.

"The fire also produced a hero. Gus Brazzle, a uniformed security officer from Justice Security here in the city, was assigned to the bookstore. The store clerk's five-year-old daughter had become trapped inside the store. Mr. Brazzle bravely went back into the burning building to rescue the child. We have dramatic video of that rescue, which we will show you now. But, we must warn you, the scenes are very graphic, and parental guidance is urged..."

Two weeks after the fire, a memorial was held at the Justice Security building. Three hundred of the over four hundred employees attended.

When Gus's will had been found, it was discovered that he had left his house and all of his worldly goods to Nicole, with Teresa as executor. Misty had seen to it that Justice Security had also set up a trust fund to ensure Nicole's future.

Teresa and Nicole came to the memorial. Both cried when Misty talked about Gus's bravery and unselfish act to save one little girl...to give her a chance at a good life.

And hanging on the memorial wall at Justice Security is a shadowbox containing Gus Brazzle's badge...and a small stuffed teddy bear holding a packet of sugar.

SATURDAY IN THE PARK

A JUSTICE SECURITY SHORT STORY

The bullet went past with a loud *ZING!* Percival "King Louie" Washington ducked his head as the bullet ricocheted off the bathroom bricks behind him. He was crouched behind a half wall that led to the bathrooms in the brick building behind him. Louie was seeking cover from the shooting war going on in the city's main park.

"Damn!" he said out loud. *This is all Misty's fault! 'Let's have the Justice Security partner meeting as a picnic in the city park this year' she sez...it'll be great!' Damn her perky little self, and damn this picnic, too! Shoulda stayed home in bed, relaxin'!* These thoughts ran through his mind in seconds. Out loud, he again said, "Damn!"

Louie stuck his head up to take a look, and a bullet hit the half wall in front of him, throwing shattered pieces of brick and mortar into his face. He ducked back down quickly.

"Louie! Are you okay, man? Answer me!" squawked Louie's radio.

Louie shook his head a couple of times trying to clear it. When he did, he keyed his radio. "Yeah, Joey, I'm fine. Little bit of brick got me in the face is all."

"I saw it. That was close. Too close."

"Who *are* these assholes, Joey?" asked Louie.

"They could belong to the Giambini family," said Joey Justice. Justice Security had made enemies of the Giambini crime family when the family had kidnapped Jacqueline Belew. The foster kids in Belew's care had hired Justice Security to find her. In the resulting chaos, Justice Security had retrieved Belew...but the Giambini family had put a price on Joey's head. "They're still after me...but I'm not sure." A shot rang out, and over Louie's radio, he heard Joey say, "Dammit!"

"You sure, man?" asked Louie. "You don't think it's Fernandez again, do you?" Justice Security had also made a mortal enemy of Esteban Fernandez, the insane Mexican general who also controlled one of the biggest drug cartels in the world. He, too, had put a huge bounty not just on Joey's head, but on all of the partners.

"Honestly, Louie? I don't have a clue *who* they are!"

Another voice came across the radio. "Joey, I think Megan and I can give you some cover fire, if you want to find better cover," said Dexter Beck.

Joey Justice, head of Justice Security, was crouched down behind a garbage can and an overturned picnic table. A huge open field full of running families was behind him. In front of him was a footpath leading to a wooded area, with an overhead bridge crossing it that serviced another footpath. The shooters were all spread out along the footpaths, woods, and bridge, utilizing every bit of good cover offered. Joey, Louie, Dexter, and Dexter's wife, Megan, were the only four partners in the park at the moment. The ambush had been obviously planned, and was very fortuitous for the shooters. They had the best cover, and the Justice Security partners had to scramble for what little cover they could find.

It was Saturday, and the park was full of families enjoying a beautiful spring day. When Misty Wilhite, partner and Joey Justice's fiancé, suggested that they have this year's meeting as a 'partner picnic' at the park, all six of the partners agreed.

Misty, along with Jessica Queen, the sixth partner in the company, was picking up food and supplies for the picnic, while the other four were to find a suitable location – a table, if they could find an open one, or a blanket on the ground if they couldn't. As they walked through the park, Louie had split off to go to the bathroom, and that's when the shooting started. Louie broke into a run to hide behind the half wall, Joey flipped over a picnic table next to a garbage can, and the Becks, Dexter and Megan, took shelter behind a fireplace inside an open-walled pavilion. An ice cream pushcart had been on the footpath, and a hotdog cart, but the vendors were long gone...no one saw where they went, but the carts were still there. There also had been a man making helium balloon animals on the footpath about halfway between the partners and the shooters. When he realized that he was in both lines of fire, he began running across the open field located behind Joey, as did the many people in the park.

Now, whoever was shooting at them, Joey understood that there were a couple of really good shots among them. He estimated that there were five or so, and said so on his radio.

"I think you're right, man," agreed Louie.

"Joey," said Megan. "I see a sixth one. He's in a tree about sixty yards in front of you. He has a rifle with a scope."

"Damn!" said Joey under his breath. *Too far for a decent shot with a handgun. It could be done, but I'm not that good.*

Into the radio, he said, "Well, friends, I'm open to suggestions."

"I wish they'd stop. I gotta piss," said Louie. He could hear his friends laughing across the grass.

"Sure you didn't piss yourself, big guy?" asked Dexter.

Louie keyed his radio. "C'mere, Dex, I'll show *you* how to piss yourself!" More laughter.

Louie wondered again at the fact that they were cracking jokes under a pressure situation ...he had gotten into a conversation about that very thing with Dr. Caleb Mitchell, the Justice Security staff psychiatrist. Caleb had said that it was a release mechanism, and that in stressful situations, the joking was used to relieve some of that stress, and to draw them closer to each other in order to present a united front.

"Really?" Louie had asked.

Caleb had nodded. "Either that, or you're the most immature bunch of morons I've *ever* worked with!"

Louie wished Caleb was here with them right now. He'd welcome the opportunity to hear Caleb crack a few jokes. *And shoot a couple of bad guys while he's at it.*

Joey had been peeking through the cracks between boards on the picnic table, and between the picnic table and garbage can. The shooter with the rifle worried him. From that distance, and with a rifle, he'd be able to pick off each of the partners easily, if they were in the open. The rifleman was uphill from Joey and the others, and twenty feet up, sitting on a tree branch. Joey studied the layout of their positions, and the attackers' positions. He discovered that if he moved to his right just a little bit, and kept as low as possible, the five-foot-tall helium tank that the balloon guy had left behind would keep the man in the tree from having a clear shot.

Joey keyed his radio. "Dexter, Megan, you there?"

The answer came right back. "We're here," said Dexter.

"I've found a way to give myself a bit of cover from the guy with the rifle. I need you two closer to Louie and I, so I'm going to start firing a few rounds toward the shooters. The sniper won't have a clear shot at me, but he'll certainly be watching for one. While he's watching me, it should give you two a chance to move up."

"Save me a couple to shoot at, would you?" asked Megan.

Joey smiled. "I'm sure they'll still be here, Rambo." He took one last look as he moved into position.

"You two be careful," said Louie.

Joey counted to three to himself, and moved his head slightly above the picnic table. He had been right – he couldn't see the rifleman, and the rifleman couldn't see him. Joey took aim, and fired his weapon, carefully placing his shots at bits of likely cover.

Louie could see the man with the rifle, however. The man kept looking through his scope, trying to get a clear shot at Joey. Finally, just as Dexter and Megan reached cover with Joey, the rifleman could stand it no longer. He squeezed off a shot toward Joey. The shot hit the nozzle and control valve on top of the helium tank and loosened them. The force of the shot also pushed the helium tank just enough so that it began to fall from the hill it was placed on. The top of the tank fell toward Joey, and the nozzle and valve hit a rock on the ground as it fell, breaking them off. The helium tank had just been filled, and the pressurized gas released at just the right speed to propel the tank up the small hill. At the top of the hill, the tank became airborne, and the tank's angle and trajectory carried it directly to the man in the tree. It hit him solidly, and knocked him out of the tree. He fell the twenty feet to the ground, and didn't move.

Louie began talking into his radio. "We are the luckiest four people on the face of this earth! Did you *see* that shit? It was like a cartoon, man! And Joey didn't even blow that tank up – it was the other guy!"

Joey was still shaking his head, not believing what he had seen, and laughing at what his friend was saying on the radio.

Dexter had chosen to stay on Joey's left side, behind the picnic table. Dexter's wife, Megan, had found cover behind the trash can on Joey's right.

Once the shooters realized that their man in the tree was out of the equation, the shooters began firing a flurry of shots in anger toward Joey's position. A couple of shots had even penetrated the wood of the picnic table, and left neat little holes that could be peeked through without exposing oneself. The shots slowed considerably after the first twenty or so.

"Guys, I have a dumb question," said Megan. "Before I ask, remember that I'm including myself in this, too. Why haven't any of us used our cell phones?

We could call Misty and Jessica, and warn them. And we could also call for backup."

Joey looked at Megan with one eyebrow raised. "Backup? When there's only five bad guys?" He shook his head. "The day us four can't handle five shooters is the day we need to retire!"

"Six, Joey," replied Megan. "You only got lucky with number six."

Dexter was shaking his head. "That couldn't have gone better if we'd planned it. I still don't believe that it happened!"

Joey dug his cell phone out of his pocket. "That *was* pretty cool, wasn't it? I felt like the Road Runner for a minute." He tapped Misty's number from his contacts list and waited for her to answer. "Would one of you please let Louie know that I'm calling Misty?"

Louie chose that moment to fire off a couple of shots, then his voice came to them on the radio. "Hey, I hate to break up your little *soiree*, but I just drove one back that was trying to make it to the hot dog stand. I don't think he was hongry, do you?"

Joey laughed as Misty answered her phone. "Hi, sweet man! Have you chosen a good spot for our picnic?"

A bullet hit the top of the picnic table and ricocheted away. "We've got a spot here, but I'm not sure that it's good. Misty, we are pinned down by approximately five shooters not far into the park. They ambushed us, and we don't know who they are."

"Oh, my God!" Misty replied. "Is anyone hurt?"

"Only a man with a rifle. He was hit by a helium tank."

Misty was silent for a moment. "A *helium* tank?"

Joey smiled and shook his head. "You had to be here...oh, and Louie's face got sprayed with a few shards of brick when a bullet hit the bathroom wall."

Another few seconds of silence. "Joey, are you guys drinking already? I mean, Jessica and I were bringing some beer, but..."

Joey had peeked over the top of the picnic table, and he saw one of the shooters running from left to right. The ambusher was trying to get better cover. Holding the phone with his left hand and his Glock with his right, he squeezed off two well-aimed shots, aiming for the man's legs. Both shots hit their target, and the man fell in plain sight of the Justice Security group.

"Don't kill him!" Joey called out to Louie. "We need somebody we can question."

Misty had heard the entire exchange. "Joey, hold on!" she said urgently. "Jessica and I are coming!"

The downed man started calling to his partners, in what sounded like German.

German? thought Joey. *Who did we piss off that speaks German?* "Misty, will you please call Marcus?" Marcus Moore was the FBI liaison to Justice Security. "I just heard one of these guys speaking German. I was thinking that they might be some of Giambini's people, but none of them are German! We'll need help questioning survivors and identifying them."

The wounded man was still moaning and calling out in German. Finally, someone from the ambushers' side fired a single shot. The wounded man's head snapped back, and he collapsed onto the ground.

"I didn't do that, Joe!" called Louie. "*They* did!"

"I *know,* dammit!" Into the phone, he said, "They just shot the wounded man that was speaking German." He gave her their location in the park.

"We'll be there in about five minutes, Joey. Stay safe!"

Joey disconnected the call. To Dexter and Megan, he said tonelessly, "She said to stay safe." The three were silent for a few seconds, then all three burst out laughing.

Suddenly, shots began coming from the ambushers' area, and were aimed not only at Joey's cover, but at Louie's as well.

They could hear shouting from the other side as they were shooting. "*Schnell! Schnell!*"

Joey's radio spoke with Louie's voice again. "I can't get a shot off! They're covering one of them, and he's heading for the hot dog cart again!"

Obviously, the man had made it safely, because the shooting had stopped.

Dexter said, "Look, somebody's got to take that guy out. I'm the logical one, because I'm so quiet on my feet. Here's what I plan: Megan, you give me cover fire toward the bad guys. Joey, you fire a few shots toward the hot dog stand. I'll run to cover with Louie – it's a straight shot from here – and then, we'll decide the best way for me to get to him. How's that?"

Megan was nodding. Joey knew that Dexter was right, and they had to do something. Finally, he nodded.

"Get ready, Dex." To Megan, Joey said, "On three. One...two...*three!*" Megan, using two handguns, began shooting toward the footpath and bridge. Joey began shooting at the hot dog stand. Dexter began running full tilt to Louie's position at the bathroom.

Joey's shots broke the mustard container, and sprayed mustard all over the cart. Another broke the glass surrounding the hot dog wheel. A third shot sprayed hot dog buns all over the stand and the area around the stand.

Megan called out, "I got one!"

Joey turned his head slightly as he responded. "Great!" He turned back to the hot dog stand, and saw movement behind it. Someone's head ducked down below the line of sight. Joey aimed lower, toward the wooden base of the stand, and squeezed off a couple of shots, hoping they would penetrate the wood and wound the assailant.

Instead, one of the two shots hit the propane tank that the hot dog vendor used to cook the hot dogs. The propane tank exploded, and blew the hot dog stand apart. The concussion from the explosion blew Joey and Megan onto their backs. Flames from the explosion climbed fifteen feet into the air, and the wood base that was the stand's foundation burned merrily. Cries of "*Scheisse!*" could be heard from the bridge over the footpath. Dexter had made it to the safety of the half wall an instant before the stand exploded, and both he and Louie ducked down to avoid the blast.

As Joey and Megan picked themselves up, pieces of the hot dog stand were still falling around them. Some of the pieces were on fire, and some were not.

Megan started laughing. "Joey...you did it again!"

After a few seconds, Joey began laughing with her. "I didn't even think about that stand having anything explosive!" Joey had a reputation for accidentally blowing things up.

"Hey, Joey!" called Dexter. "If you wanted that guy for yourself, you should have called 'dibs'!"

Megan began laughing harder, and Joey could hear Dexter and Louie laughing, too.

"Hey!" yelled Joey. "Notice anything?"

The other three looked around.

"Nobody's shooting at us!" said Louie.

"Think they're gone?" asked Dexter.

Megan answered him. "Honey pooh, if our count was right, there should only have been two left: The helium tank got one, the shooters shot their own man, I shot one giving you cover to get to Louie, and Joey blew one up. That's four that were taken out. Even I would have to think twice about odds like that."

The three men and the lady slowly stood. As they were surveying the area, Joey heard a voice.

"Honey! We brought you something!"

The speaker was Misty Wilhite. With her was Jessica Queen, and both ladies had handguns aimed at two men walking in front of them. Both men were blond, around thirty, and one man wore glasses. Their hands were laced together on top of their heads.

"Were you looking for these guys, fearless leader?" asked Jessica.

The ladies stopped in front of the bathroom. To their prisoners, Jessica said, "On your knees, gentlemen...*NOW!*"

The men got onto their knees.

"Hands behind your backs, please...and oh, soooo slowly," said Misty.

Slowly, the men put their hands behind their backs, and Misty put cuffs on both as the partners all gathered around the two prisoners.

Misty said, "Louie, would you please go cuff the man beside the helium tank? He's broken, but he's alive."

The prisoner with the glasses muttered, "*Scheisse.*"

Joey nudged the man with his foot, and said, "I *really* don't want to hear you talk right now." To the others he said, raising his voice so Louie could hear, too, "Anybody recognize these guys?"

"I do," said Marcus Moore. He had just moved up to them, with his weapon pointed in the air. "The gentleman with the glasses is Hans Krause. He's a mercenary and small-time arms dealer...from Germany."

"Hi, Marcus!" said Joey. "Glad you could join us! How did you know where to find us in the park?"

Marcus smiled ruefully. "I just followed the smoke...figured it had to be you."

Megan started laughing again. "That's our Joey!"

LATER, WITH THE PARK full of FBI men prowling around, Joey and the other partners were talking with Marcus.

"The man that fell from the tree sang like a bird," said Marcus. "I told him that there wouldn't be any medical help for him until he told me what I wanted to know." He looked at Joey. "Your radios are compromised. They had radios, and that's how they knew you'd be here today – they heard you all talking about it. You might want to talk to this guy." He handed Joey a card. "His company makes encrypted radios. Best bet for private communication. Anyway, they don't belong to either Fernandez, or the Giambini family. They're mercenaries, looking purely for the paycheck from capturing you. That *is* quite a chunk of change, you know...and it's dead or alive."

The sober looks on the partners' faces told the story. They were amazed that this entire thing had happened, and even more amazed at the reason.

Misty looked at Joey and said, "I just can't take you anywhere, can I?"

They all chuckled, but the meaning was clear: With a bounty on not just Joey's head, but on everyone else's too, it was going to be difficult to keep their business going.

Beyond the yellow crime scene tape, a small crowd had gathered. Among them was Miriam Apple from Channel 7 News, who called out to Joey. Beside her was Steve, her ever-present cameraman.

"Wow," he said. "Let me go talk to her for a just a minute, then we'll all head home. Anybody want to join me?"

Marcus shook his head, but the other partners joined him. They walked over to Miriam, and exchanged pleasantries.

"I have a couple of questions, Joey," said Miriam.

"Go ahead."

Steve nodded.

"With me are Joey Justice and the other partners of Justice Security. Joey, what happened here today?"

"Well, some bad people tried to ambush us...," Joey began, and told a brief synopsis of the shootout.

The next question caught Joey by surprise.

"This is for all of the partners: Many of the city's residents are frightened of what is happening. What is your reaction to the accusation that Justice Security has now become a danger to this city?"

Joey was dumbfounded, and speechless.

Louie quickly took over. "All I can say is, we have no control over what bad guys do in this city. All we can do is assure folks that we'll keep them as safe as we can. That's our promise to the citizens of this city!"

As the group began walking in the direction of their cars, Miriam said, "One last question: How did today's events make you feel?"

The partners stopped, and looked at each other.

Louie turned to Miriam and said, "Just another Saturday in the park, Miriam."

The partners again began moving toward their cars, their minds focused on one

thing: home.

MACARTHUR PARK

A JUSTICE SECURITY SHORT STORY

Megan Beck assembled her equipment and contemplated how she got roped into this particular assignment.

It was three days ago, she thought to herself. *Joey did it.*

Megan completed the assembly of the automatic weapon that had been waiting for her. She inserted the clip holding the ammunition, put her hand on the other piece of equipment that was there for her, and waited for her cue to come out shooting.

I love shooting things up, and eliminating bad guys, but I don't even know what's going on!

Two days earlier, Megan and her husband, Dexter, were working in the Justice Security computer lab on the second sub-basement level in the Justice Security Building. As the resident Information Technology experts, they were working with their computer teams, building a top- secret, computer-driven, remote security system for a local government entity, when the phone on the desk rang. Megan answered.

"Hey, Rambo!" said Percival "King Louie" Washington. "Lemme talk to Dex, please...we got some workin' out to do."

Megan smiled at her friend and partner. "Sure, Louie, hold on a minute." She handed the phone to Dexter. He spoke to Louie for a moment, then hung up.

"Honey, I'm going to work out with Louie for a while. He needs more training from his sensei." Dexter was also the martial arts expert for the company, having spent many years in his youth training with various masters.

"Be home for dinner?" she asked.

Doing his best Spock imitation, Dexter replied, "It would be illogical to leave the prepared meal uneaten. I shall arrive at the appointed time."

With a smile, Megan replied cheerfully, "Blow it out your ass, dear. See you at six."

Dexter kissed her, and headed upstairs to the gym.

A little later, Megan decided to wrap up, and head upstairs to the apartment she shared with her husband. The Justice Security building had apartments on the fifth and sixth aboveground floors, for partners, clients needing a place to hide out for a while, or guests, like Louie's mom, Joey and Misty's parents, Dexter's brother, Jessica's dad, and Megan's grandmother.

Megan checked out the work the rest of the IT team was doing, made a couple of suggestions, left a couple of instructions, and headed for the elevators.

The elevator dinged for the first floor, which contained the cafeteria, staff locker rooms, medical offices for both Dr. Orville Eugene ("Call me Buddy") Bishop and Dr. Caleb Mitchell. Dr. Bishop was the staff doctor/surgeon, and Dr. Mitchell was the staff psychiatrist. The lobby also housed the main desk, which was directed by Tony Armstrong, and the mailroom. Tony was the head of the grunts, the uniformed members of Justice Security, and, along with Mark Haase, coordinated the uniformed assignments. Main desk duties also included mailroom duties, such as x-raying suspicious packages and distributing incoming mail. Misty Wilhite oversaw the grunts, and was the partner that Tony answered to directly.

When the elevator doors slid open, Joey Justice put his hand against the elevator door as he finished his conversation with Charlie Li, a plainclothes security officer that worked mostly with Dexter and Jessica.

"Think you can do that, Charlie?" asked Joey.

"Yes, sir, I can take care of that with no problem," answered Charlie, who also waved to Megan. "Hi, Megan!"

Megan smiled and waved back. "Hi, Charlie!"

Joey smiled at Charlie and said, "Thanks, Charlie. Remember: Top Secret!"

"Yes, sir, Joey!"

Joey climbed aboard the elevator, saw that Megan had already pressed "6", and leaned against the elevator wall.

"Something going on?" asked Megan.

Joey nodded. "Yeah. It's top secret stuff, though. Partners are in on it only on need-to-know. Orders."

Megan nodded. It didn't happen often, but occasionally, an assignment came in from their FBI liaison, Marcus Moore, that the partners were kept on a need-to-know basis. Joey tried hard to shy away from those, because he felt that every partner should know everything about every case, should something happened to the partner overseeing a particular case. In that instance, another partner could step up and take over without a lot of explanation. Marcus argued that if something happened to the need-to-know partner, that Marcus himself could bring another partner up to speed. The money on these cases usually was very good, so Joey took on more of them than he liked.

Joey looked at Megan. "Actually, Megan, you may be able to do something for this particular case, if you don't ask questions about your assignment."

Megan shrugged. "I'll do what I can, Joe...I always do. And I won't ask questions. I figure you'll tell me anything I *need* to know."

"You'll have to keep it from Dexter, too...can you do that?"

"Of course."

Joey nodded. "Okay, then, give me a couple of days, and I'll get back to you with your assignment."

"Sure." Megan thought for a minute. "Hey, wait a minute! Will I be done in time to celebrate Dexter's birthday? It's three days from now, and Dexter's brother is going to be here."

Joey shrugged. "I know, Megan, and I'll do what I can, but no promises. This job is pretty important. If it's any consolation, it looks like I'll be busy on Dexter's birthday, too."

The elevator stopped at the sixth floor, and both Joey and Megan got out and went to their separate apartments.

Yes, that was it. Three days ago, and, of course, I'm missing my husband's birthday. Joey promised to explain it to him. I hope he didn't forget it, or I'll get Misty to give him hell about it!

These thoughts went through Megan's head as she waited, watching light fading in and out through the cracks of whatever it was that contained her. At least she could breathe, although the cracks weren't big enough to see through, they did allow the occasional light to pass through, as they rumbled through the city's streets to her destination.

Damn Joey. Didn't even tell me where I'm going, either.

A trickle of uneasy sweat ran down the center of Megan's back.

Two days later, Megan was again working in the computer lab when the phone rang.

"Computer lab, this is Megan."

"Hi, 'this-is-Megan'. This is Joey. Can you come to my office?"

"Can you give me five minutes?"

"Sure."

"Thanks. Be there in a jif." She hung up.

Five minutes later, after she had gotten to a stopping point, she shut down her computer and headed to the elevators. Once inside, she pressed the button for the fourth floor.

In the Justice Security building, the fourth floor housed the partner offices, a conference room for clients, and the situation room. It also was Turk Wendall's workplace.

Formerly, Turk Wendell had been Louie Washington's right hand man. Turk was a huge, hulking man, with a dark chocolate complexion. And, much to everyone's surprise, he was very adept with secretarial skills. Turk's massive hands dwarfed a computer keyboard, but his fingers flew across one. Some said that he was faster than Jessica Queen had ever been. Jessica had once been the executive secretary, but had accepted an offered partnership. Her replacement, Patti Hoehn, had been kidnapped and killed by Justice Security's mortal enemy, Esteban Fernandez. Turk had taken the job after that, and had been great at it.

So, when the elevator doors slid open on the fourth floor, Turk was sitting with his hand underneath the desk. It was resting on the hidden Glock aimed at the elevators. When he saw that the visitor was Megan, he removed his hand, jerked his head in the direction of Joey's office, and said, "Waitin' for you."

"Thanks, Turk," she replied.

Turk grunted.

Megan knocked on Joey's door as she went in. Joey was sitting behind his desk. His fiancé and Justice Security partner, Misty Wilhite, was standing behind him, bent over his shoulder. Their FBI liaison, Marcus Moore, was standing over Joey's other shoulder, also looking down. When Joey saw who had come in, he flipped the paper that the three had been looking at upside down on his desk, and Misty stood up.

"Hi, Megan," said Misty.

"Hi, Marcus. Hi, Misty," replied Megan.

Joey indicated the chair across the desk from him. "Have a seat."

"Thanks. What's going on?" asked Megan.

Joey looked up at Marcus, letting him take over. Marcus smiled a small smile, and did just that.

"Misty," said Marcus. "Can you assemble a machine pistol in the dark, by feel alone?"

Misty guffawed. "Of course! Nothing to it!"

Marcus shook his head. "All these years with the Bureau, and I still can't do it. Not by feel alone. Amazing."

"It just takes a little practice, Marcus. Anyone can do it. Dexter can do it, too...and faster than I can. Louie and I are about the same speed. I don't know about Jessica. Or Joey and Misty, for that matter."

Marcus shook his head again. "I still say it's amazing. Okay, I know Joey mentioned a case to you a couple of days ago, right?"

"He did."

"If you're still willing to help, I have your assignment."

Damn! Megan thought. *It's Dexter's birthday, and I gotta go be Rambo again!* Out loud, she said, "Okay. What do I need to do?"

Marcus smiled. "At six o'clock tonight, you'll meet us in the lobby, and we'll take you down to the employee garage. I'll blindfold you, give you a simple timer, and lead you to a small enclosed container. The container is attached to an SUV, which will drive you to the destination. The SUV will park. While riding to the destination, you will assemble the machine pistol I spoke to you about. The other piece of equipment is a simple audio device, connected to an amplifier inside the container. Once parked, you will wait inside for the timer I will have given you to go off. Once it goes off, you will open the top of the container, and stand up. Once standing, you will fire your weapon into the air, then press the button on the audio device. The audio will be instructions for you, and for the target. You will do what the instructions tell you, then you will wait for extraction. Any questions, Megan?"

Megan thought. "Who is the target?"

"Classified."

Megan frowned a bit. "May I at least know the destination?"

"Classified. I've told you all that I can, Megan," replied Marcus.

Megan looked at Joey. He met her gaze and shrugged, saying it was up to her.

Megan shifted her gaze to Marcus.

"Okay, I'll do it."

Megan hugged Dexter, then kissed him passionately.

"Happy birthday, my sweet husband," she said, looking deeply into his eyes. "I love you with all my heart, and I always will."

Dexter smiled at his wife. "I love you, too, Megan. You're my everything."

"I'm sorry I can't go with you to pick up Hector."

"It's okay, honey. You have to finish that security program, so I'll see you later."

Megan thought, *I hope so.*

Riding in the container, something started dripping steadily on Megan's head. She looked up at the crack in the container.

She thought, *Oh, great...it's starting to rain. Why couldn't they have made this thing waterproof?*

Marcus and Joey met Megan in the building's lobby.

"Right on time," said Marcus.

"Riiiiiggghhttt," responded Megan.

Joey shook his head. "Megan, you don't have to do this if you don't want to."

Megan shook her head. "No, I said I would, and I'm going to. Let's do it."

Marcus produced a blindfold. It was one of those that people use when they're sleeping, to keep out light. "You're on, then, lady." He twirled his finger in the air. "Mind turning around?"

Megan turned her back to the two men, and dropped her purse on the floor. "Joey, would you please see that my purse gets taken to our apartment?"

"I will," said Joey.

Marcus put the blindfold on Megan, then turned her around and checked to make sure that she couldn't see.

"I'm sorry to be so thorough, Megan. It's imperative that you can't see anything."

"I understand, Marcus."

"Once you're inside the container, and it's well underway, you can remove the mask."

Megan nodded. "I will, Marcus."

"It's time to go," said Joey.

Megan couldn't see a thing. She heard the elevator doors open, and one of the men guided her onto it by gently holding her arm. She felt the elevator descending one floor. When it stopped, she heard he elevator doors open. Again she was led a few steps.

"Okay, Megan. If you reach out, you can feel the sides of the entrance to the container," said Marcus.

Megan reached out, and felt the blunt metallic edges of the entrance.

"You'll need to duck your head to climb in," Marcus told her.

Megan felt for the top of the entrance, found it, and climbed into the container without any problems.

She felt something put into her hand. It was about the size of a small pocket calculator.

Marcus said, "This is your timer. It's preset, and I just pressed the button for the countdown. When it goes off, please do as I instructed you earlier. You'll pop up through the extra hatch in the top."

Megan nodded. "Will do, Marcus. Joey?"

"Yes, Megan?"

"If I don't make it back..."

Megan could hear the smile in Joey's voice. "You'll make it back."

Megan nodded once. "Then, I'm ready to go." She heard the container door being secured.

"Good luck, and enjoy yourself."

Megan heard the remark, but the voice was so muffled that she couldn't tell which man said it.

Now, the dripping had become steadier, and Megan could actually hear it hitting the top of the container.

She was soaked.

Suddenly, Megan felt the SUV decelerating until it stopped moving, then it accelerated again into a left turn. She heard the timer rattling across the floor as the left turn continued.

Nothing I can do about that now...if it breaks, I'll just have to wing it. My hands are full.

The SUV went over a bump, then felt as if it were going downhill. *Must be going down a slope.*

The downhill feeling leveled out, and the SUV began slowing, then stopped. Megan heard the driver's door slam shut.

Through the thin metal making up the container, she could hear voices. They were counting something down.

"FIVE...FOUR...THREE...TWO...ONE!"

Megan's timer began beeping.

Oh, crap, this is it! She began hyperventilating. After ten deep breaths, Megan unfastened the top hatch and stood up.

Once outside the container, Megan aimed her weapon into the air at an angle, and fired into the air, emptying the clip. She noticed that a spotlight had been aimed at her, and that there was total silence in whatever room she was in.

Megan pressed the "play" button on the audio device.

Music began playing. The tune was "The Stripper", performed by David Rose and his orchestra.

From behind Megan, catcalls and shouts of "Happy Birthday" could be heard over the music.

Megan whirled around. Ten feet away, on the floor of a large lunchroom-type eating area, was Dexter. He was surrounded by almost everyone from Justice Security. Marcus Moore was there, and was laughing so hard that his hands were holding his stomach, and tears were rolling down his face. Joey Justice stood close to Dexter, and was laughing almost as hard as Marcus. Louie was patting Dexter on the back. Dexter's brother, Hector, was standing next to Dexter. Hector had a surprised look on his face. Misty stood with Joey, and was smirking. When Misty saw that Megan had seen her, Misty waved. Jessica Queen was standing beside Louie, smiling and shaking her head, as if she couldn't believe that they had pulled such a stunt.

Megan looked down, and realized that she was inside a huge, fake, painted birthday cake, with fake, green-painted icing that was melting down the sides of the cake, and causing green puddles underneath the trailer on which the cake was sitting.

Big letters on the back of the room said, "Douglas MacArthur Park Meeting Hall".

"The Stripper" was still playing through the hidden speakers of the cake's audio system.

Megan shrugged, and began doing a striptease along with the music. Each piece of clothing was thrown to the audience: Dexter. He was the only audience that Megan was concerned with. She timed the striptease so that she was only in bra and panties when the music ended. She climbed off of the cake, walked over to her husband, and hugged him tightly.

"Happy Birthday, Dexter," she whispered in his ear. "I guess the surprise was for both of us!"

Dexter hugged Megan close with his eyes closed. He was fighting back tears, although only Megan could tell. "It's the best birthday I've ever had, lover...and I just got the best gift that could have been given."

When the couple finally separated from their hug, Joey and Marcus were standing there.

"I hope you two aren't mad at us," said Joey.

"Yeah, it wasn't easy pulling this off," added Marcus.

"Everyone was in on it except you two...and Hector, of course," Joey said. "But no one wanted to try to help us. They were afraid Megan would blow her top."

"We wanted to surprise both of you," Marcus said. "We thought a surprise party in the Justice Security building would be too easy to figure out. That's why we rented the MacArthur Park Meeting Hall."

Both Megan and Dexter began laughing. Then they started hugging their friends, and thanking them.

Later, after the birthday party was over and Megan and Dexter were back home, the couple began a small celebration of their own. Hector had chosen to stay in one of the guest suites on the fifth floor, rather than intrude on the couple on Dexter's birthday.

During pillow talk, Dexter quipped, "Well, I'm glad I salvaged that 'cake' that was left out in the rain."

"You'd *better* have salvaged it," Megan replied. "You won't ever find *this* recipe again!"

"I love you, Megan."

"I love you back, Dexter."

THE LITTLE DRUMMER BOY

A JUSTICE SECURITY SHORT STORY

"What's the big secret about Christmas Eve, guys?" asked Megan Beck. She had directed her question to her husband and partner, Dexter Beck, and to one of her other partners in Justice Security, Percival "King Louie" Washington.

Justice Security was the most successful security company in the city, founded by four friends from college: Joey Justice, Misty Wilhite, Dexter Beck, and Louie Washington. Two more partners had recently joined the four original partners as full partners in the company: Jessica Queen, and Megan Fisk Beck.

It was Christmas Eve, and it was the first Christmas Eve that Megan had spent as Megan Beck. She and Dexter were still considered newlyweds.

It was nine o'clock on the night before Christmas. Dexter and Louie had invited Megan to come with them to their destination. Both were very reticent about telling her where they were going.

"Wait until we get in the car, Megan," Dexter had said. "I promise that Louie and I will explain the meaning of tonight to you then."

Now, in the car, driving through a lightly falling snow that hadn't begun sticking to the ground quite yet, Megan asked her question again.

"Tell me why we're out on Christmas Eve, and what's so secret about it?"

Dexter, who was driving, looked in the rear view mirror into Louie's eyes. "You start, Louie. You're the one it began with anyway."

Louie smiled. "Sure thing, little buddy." He leaned back into his seat, a huge, muscular man with coffee-colored skin, and began his story.

Back then, Justice Security was just starting out. Joey took any job that came along...well, he still does that, doesn't he? But, we took any kind of job, from providin' security, to uniformed guards, to private detective services, to bodyguarding VIPs.

That particular night we had contracted to provide armed security escort and bodyguard protection to this famous band that was performing here in the city. There were three members of the band, and I was guarding the drummer, Gil Mullins. Joey had the lead guitar player, and Misty had the other guy...I forget what he played in the band.

Anyhow, this band – Omega – was playing a special charity gig in the convention center downtown.

"Omega?" interrupted Megan. "They were *huge!* And Justice Security was their bodyguards?"

"You bet we were, and we were proud of it, too," answered Louie.

"That was the first year we were in business," added Dexter. "So, yeah, it was a big thing for us then."

"Oh, man, I would have loved to have met Gil Mullins," said Megan. "I loved his work with Omega, and I loved his solo work, too."

"You wanna hear this story, or not, Megan?" asked Louie.

"I'm sorry," Megan answered sheepishly. "Please go ahead."

Anyway, I had the responsibility of taking care of the drummer, Gil Mullins. I was young then, and really wanted to impress the man with my abilities, so I was all for goin' by the book.

Omega had received some death threats, and their manager wanted to make sure that nothing happened to them while they were in the city. We didn't have as many people then as we do now, so we all had to do our part. And with a contract this big, we took it upon ourselves to make sure it was done *right*.

The concert was supposed to start at eight o'clock, which meant that we had to have the band members at the convention center no later than seven-thirty.

Joey had decided to split the band up, and each of us would arrive separately with our assigned band member. I believe Tony Armstrong had come on board by then, and so had Jessica, as the "executive secretary". They were keeping things under control at the office, so Dexter tagged along with me.

The band was staying at Embassy Suites wayyyy out by the airport. We left early, so that we could be at the hotel by five o'clock. It was snowing – had been for a couple of hours – and the snow had stacked up to about two inches. We didn't think anything of it, because it wasn't that bad. The streets were still mostly clear. When we got to the hotel, we went inside, found the manager and the head of the band's permanent security, and let them know that we were in place. We could leave whenever they were ready to go.

Omega's manager told us to just sit tight in the lobby until the band members were ready. The plan was to leave the hotel by six forty-five to give us plenty of time to get to the convention center.

Maaannn, that was the best hour and a half I'd spent in a long time! The four of us just sittin' there, talkin' and bullshittin', just like we used to back in college...it was good times!

Come six-thirty, and the band members came to the lobby with their manager and the head of their security. We shook hands all around, decided who would ride with who, and headed for the front door of the hotel.

It had been snowing a lot since we went inside. It had risen to about six inches by then, and the streets had about four inches. The hotel clerk told us that a blizzard was due to hit any time, and that the snow could pile up to over a foot.

"I remember that year!" exclaimed Megan. "It was one of the worst blizzards ever to hit the city!" She shook her head. "And you guys were out in it. Amazing."

"We were definitely in it," said Dexter. "That night, we found out that snow isn't something to play with. Go ahead, Louie."

We told the band that going out was up to them. If they wanted to go, we'd take them.

They discussed it amongst themselves, and decided to go ahead and perform. It was Christmas Eve, and the concert was for charity, so they felt obligated.

We loaded up. Joey had the manager and the lead guitar player, Misty had the middle guy and the head of their security, and Dex and I had Gil Mullins. The rest of their staff security people were already at the convention center.

Joey, for safety's sake, had us all taking separate routes to the concert, which, in hindsight, turned out to be kinda stupid, but we didn't think so at the time. Our cars were front wheel drive, so we weren't too worried about getting through the city streets. But we shoulda been.

The three of us did okay, for a while. We had to take it slow. We hadn't been away from the hotel for ten minutes when the blizzard hit. Forty mile an hour winds, more snow than I've ever seen, and it didn't take long for the snow to accumulate to the bumper on the front of the car. We couldn't see shit! The only way we knew that we were even still on the street was because of the buildings on either side. I think we actually drove on the sidewalk in a couple of spots. The temperature had dropped to about ten degrees, and the snow was blinding.

Just as we hit Hooker Hollow, the worst happened. The power went out all over the city. The traffic lights went out, and nobody had heat anywhere. The snow had gotten so deep that we couldn't move forward anymore – the wind was blowing it so hard there were drifts as tall as me, if not taller. Dexter was driving, and we ditched the car just past McFeely's Bar.

I got to give Gil Mullins credit, though...he didn't complain, and he didn't blame us one bit. He could see what the score was, just like we did. Everything around us was locked up tight, but we couldn't stay with the car. If we stayed, we figured we'd either die of carbon monoxide poisoning, or be frozen to death. Neither choice sounded good to any of us.

We decided to leave the car, and start walking. We were only ten blocks from the convention center, and we figured we could walk that far, no matter how bad the blizzard got.

Boy, were we wrong.

We'd barely gone a block, and we were all three practically frozen solid. It was bitter cold, and so dark that we couldn't make each other out. Top it all off, we were fading fast, and we desperately needed a place to get inside, but nothing friendly was showing itself to us.

We got another half a block when we saw light shining in a window. It was real faint at first, but, as we got closer, the light seemed to be made of lots of different colors. Finally we figured out that it was the windows at St. Francis church. We headed that way.

When we got to St. Francis, we didn't have to climb any stairs to get to the door. The snow had built itself up so high, that it was right on the stoop! Somehow, we got the door open, and we fell inside.

The light had been coming from more candles than we could count. They were everywhere! Each one was giving out a faint light, but when you get that many candles going at once...well, it was almost as bright as day inside that church, but it was a warm, comforting light, too. And the heat they gave off! It was warm there...warm enough that we felt better almost right away.

Father Cantore came up the aisle, fussing over us like a mother hen. There were only about ten others inside the church besides us. We introduced ourselves to the Father, and, if he knew who Gil Mullins was, he didn't let on.

The priest ushered us to one of the rows in front, and asked if we'd like something warm to drink. We could have coffee or homemade hot chocolate. They had a small camp stove set up, with an old-fashioned coffee pot and a tea kettle sitting on it. I asked for hot chocolate, and Gil and Dexter each had coffee. I remember that so well, because about the time we had it in hand

and started to sip, the church's front door crashed open, and two more people struggled in from the storm.

Father Cantore fussed over them, too, and brought them down front, too, and asked them if they'd like somethin' hot to drink.

While the priest was getting those two something to drink, Dexter suddenly had to hit the john. He excused himself, and walked swiftly to the priest, and asked for the facilities. I don't know what he had to do, but he walked to the bathroom like somethin' was prairie-doggin'!

Well, I made a mistake while Dex was gone. See, I figured that, bein' in a church and all, we were pretty well safe. I started talkin' to Gil, and I let my guard down.

Big mistake. The next thing I knew, dey wuz a gun in my face…and it was a big one!

One of those last two folks through the door had a big old forty-four magnum, with a barrel bore big enough that you could drive a truck into, and I was lookin' right into it.

"Yeah, big man, what are you gonna do now?" the man said. "I know you thought you got away from us by ducking in here, but it didn't work, did it?"

"What are you talking about, man?" I asked.

The dude's eyes were dancin' around like firecrackers were goin' off inside him, and his friend was bouncing from foot to foot. They were nervous, and crazy, and I figured I was one dead ebony man!

"We told you in those letters, man," said the guy with the gun. "Told you we were gonna kill Gil Mullins. Tired of hearing him all over, everywhere there's a radio, or a stereo store…so we're gonna kill him!"

Now the dude was movin' that big old gun back and forth between me and Gil. His finger was on the trigger, and I couldn't reach for my gun without takin' a big risk that one of us would get shot.

Father Cantore said somthin' like, "Hey, boys, it's Christmas Eve, and this is the House of the Lord. Please put away your gun."

"*Shut the hell up, you Pope-lover!*" the man yelled at the priest, and some woman there in the church screamed.

"And, Megan, I'll let Dexter tell you the rest," finished Louie. "After all, the rest is his story."

"Yeah, thanks, big guy," said Dexter.

Okay, lover, here's the rest of it.

First, the bathroom thing. I don't know what made me want to go so urgently, but it hit me like a ton of bricks. Trouble was, when I got to the bathroom, I didn't have to do anything...no number one, no number two, not even a gas bubble to toot my own horn, so to speak. Nothing. But, I didn't want to take a chance on having an accident, so I stayed in the bathroom for a minute, trying to go. Again, nothing. Damnedest thing ever. Candles were all over the bathroom, keeping it lit and warm. I just washed my hands, and left the bathroom. I think I was shaking my head, because I couldn't believe it.

When I got back into the main part of the church, those two idiots had just told Louie that they were going to kill Gil Mullins.

The part of the church that housed the bathrooms was behind those two. They had no idea that I was there, but Father Cantore saw me.

By the time this all happened, I had just finished my training with Master Kim Po about the time we started the company, so I knew how to move stealthily. When the Father spoke to the crazy guy, that was my cue. I was as silent as the night when I jumped over the railing and hustled up behind the two.

When the woman's scream echoed away inside that huge church, I decided that enough was enough.

I said, "Excuse me, but could I get Mr. Mullins' autograph before you kill him?"

The guy with the gun whirled around, and I chopped down on his gun wrist with the heel of my hand. When it connected, the gunman's wrist went numb, and he dropped the gun. I did a spinning kick, and caught the guy on the temple. He went down and out. Still moving, I spun around to the other guy, and strong-armed his chin with my palm. I followed it with the heel of my hand to his nose, and down that guy went.

"Megan, they were the most beautiful moves I had ever seen Dexter make," interjected Louie. "And it only took seconds for him to do, but he took out both of those bad guys. I was sittin' there wonderin' why I had even come along on the trip!"

Megan giggled. "What happened then?"

"Well, both of those guys were out," said Dexter. "Father Cantore went to another part of the church, and came back with what he said were robe ties...you know, like you tie a robe with...but they were purple, so I knew that they were part of the special robes the priests wear when they're performing some service, but we still used them. Louie trussed those two up like they were cows in a rodeo."

"Didn't want those motherfu...oh, 'scuse me, Megan...*gentlemen* gettin' loose," said Louie.

"By this time, it was eleven-thirty," continued Dexter. "Father Cantore said that Christmas mass was at midnight. Gil asked the Father, since he wasn't Catholic, if he would show him how to say a thank-you prayer so that we didn't do anything sacrilegious or offensive."

"The Father told Gil that there was no 'right' way to say a prayer," said Louie. "He said that God heard 'em all, no matter what your denomination happened to be, or how you prayed, be it out loud or quiet in your head. He said that God heard what was in your heart. So, you can bet that all three of us said a prayer of thanks that night."

"The church had a nativity scene beside the altar. All three of us were on our knees beside the railing, and when Gil was through praying, he asked the Father if there might be a drum somewhere in the church," said Dexter. "Father Cantore asked him why...and Gil told him."

"Yeah," said Louie. "Gil said that for all the money he had made from his music, he didn't have a dime on him, and that the only gift he could give would be to play something on a drum."

"Father Cantore smiled at Gil's explanation, and asked Gil to come with him," continued Dexter. "The Father asked that Louie and I stay there in the church, and said that Gil would be safe with him. So, we stayed put. Five minutes later, Gil and Father Cantore came back, carrying most of a small drum set. They went back for a second trip, and brought the rest of the set. Gil spent a few minutes putting the set together, while Father Cantore prepared what he needed for the Christmas mass."

"We stayed for Christmas mass, of course," said Louie. "All three of us even took communion, at Father Cantore's insistence. He said that communion crosses several denominations, and that he couldn't give us *official* Catholic communion, but that, on *this* day, it was appropriate." Louie chuckled to himself. "First time I ever had communion with wine. I was raised a Baptist, and we always used grape juice."

"When mass was over, Father Cantore told the people in the church that Gil Mullins would perform some music to celebrate the birth of Christ. He invited Gil to come down to the altar," said Dexter. "Gil and the Father had set the drum set up beside the nativity. Megan, you have to picture this whole thing: The church was lit up solely by candlelight, the light was soft and warm, and so *intimate*. It was like we were the only people in the world, there to celebrate this child's birth."

"And the lights were even all through the church," added Louie. "Remember that, too, because nothing was lit up more than anything else."

"Gil sat down on the drum stool, and limbered his hands a bit," said Dexter. "Then he started with a beautiful rendition of 'O Come All Ye Faithful', followed with 'Do You Hear What I Hear?', and both songs were done solely with drums and Gil's acappella voice. Megan, there wasn't a sound in that church during those two songs, *except* the two songs. Then, he stopped and spoke to the congregation. He told them the same thing that he had told Father Cantore, about having nothing but his music to offer on that anniversary of the birth of Christ. And, to prove the point, he said, he would finish with the song that explained it all."

Louie shook his head. "He started playin', and the song was 'The Little Drummer Boy'."

Dexter, lost in remembering, said quietly, "Yeah. And it was fantastic."

"You may not believe what happened next, Megan, but it happened, I swear to you. Everybody in that church that night saw it," said Louie.

Both men were silent for a moment, long enough for Megan to get impatient.

"Okay, so what happened? Don't leave me hanging!" she said.

Dexter took a breath. "As Gil sang, the nativity statue of the baby Jesus began glowing softly."

"Yeah. It did. And the glow became stronger as the song went on," added Louie. "And, when Gil got to the part that says 'then he smiled at me'...well..."

"By this time, Gil had noticed it, too, and was watching the statue, so he saw it, too," said Dexter.

"*What?* What did you see?" asked Megan excitedly.

Both men took deep breaths.

Dexter said quietly, "The statue of the baby Jesus smiled. Everyone in the church saw it. He smiled at Gil...the little drummer boy."

Megan looked at her husband for several seconds. Then, she laughed. "You had me for a minute. Both of you."

"Honey, it's the truth," said Dexter.

"Whether you believe it or not, it restored the faith in every single person in that church that night...even those two nuts, who had woke up by then." Louie laughed. "Father Cantore was speechless." Louie shook his head. "Maaann, when we got rescued Christmas morning, everybody in that church had talked about what had happened. Joey, Misty, and the rest of the Omega entourage came bustin' in that morning, too. Gil had spent most of the night talking with the two nuts, and calming them down, finding out what they wanted...he refused to press charges. He told both that he would gladly pay for a psychiatrist, if they would agree to go. Of course, back then, if the client wasn't pressing charges, neither were we. There were handshakes all around, and we all left St. Francis."

"All three of us, Louie, me, and Gil Mullins...well, we made substantial donations to St. Francis Catholic Church. And we have every single year since then," said Dexter.

Louie added, "And, every single Christmas Eve, we all three go to Christmas mass at St. Francis...and Gil performs there every year."

Megan asked, "So, why haven't I ever heard about him performing there? On Christmas Eve, no less?"

Dexter smiled. "Word spread through the congregation about the 'Christmas miracle' at St. Francis...and they chose to keep quiet about Gil's involvement, and to talk about the miracle only to those that can respect it for what it is. The media would make a circus out of it. So, they keep quiet."

"Rumor has it that the Pope himself has visited St. Francis because of that night," said Louie.

"So, honey, get ready. We're here, and you're about to meet Gil Mullins," said Dexter.

"Yeah," said Louie. "And don't be surprised at some of the people you see there, either."

Louie opened the door for the Becks, and allowed them to go first. He followed, and made sure that the door closed firmly behind him.

Megan looked around as she walked into the church. Every pew was packed, the balcony was packed, and at least fifty people were standing in the background. When some members of the congregation recognized Dexter and Louie, they began applauding. Others in the congregation also began applauding, and then more, until the entire church resonated with applause for the two embarrassed security men. Megan looked at her husband with widened eyes and raised eyebrows, and she began to believe...part of their story, anyway.

Louie and Dexter waved and smiled at the congregation of St. Francis Catholic Church, embarrassed to their cores, but accepting the accolades gracefully.

Megan was indeed shocked at faces that she saw in the congregation. Miriam Apple, now the Channel 7 News Anchor/Reporter, and her courageous cameraman, Steve, waved at her from the side of the aisle.

"We're both here unofficially," Miriam said to Megan, loud enough to be heard over the applause. "Definitely *off* the record!"

Megan smiled and squeezed Miriam's hand. As she continued down the church aisle, she spotted Mayor Morris McIllwain, sitting quietly among the congregation, along with the police commissioner and the police chief. Hank McFeely and his lady bartender, Michelle, sat proudly in the middle of one pew, Hank pulling desperately at a newly purchased necktie. Many others in the church's congregation were people she recognized, and many were dressed in their "Sunday Best" and, in some cases, the "Sunday Best" was a bit run down, but clean.

Dexter pulled Megan over to a man sitting with a lady and two little girls, both about ten.

"Megan, this is Nicholas Turner," said Dexter. "He's a private investigator here in the city. He specializes in cases involving children."

Megan shook the man's hand as he said, "A real pleasure to meet you, Megan. I think Dexter and I got married about the same time. This is my wife, Meredith, and my stepdaughter, Karen."

"Pleased to meet you," said Megan. "I'm Megan Beck." She looked at the second little girl. "And what's *your* name, sweetheart?"

The second little girl said, "Madeline. But don't say anything about being able to see me. Please?" She then held her finger to her mouth in a "shushing" gesture.

Megan looked puzzled as they walked on down the aisle. Someone else stepped out to meet her, and Megan shook hands. When she looked back, still puzzled, the spot where Madeline had been sitting was empty.

Megan leaned close to Dexter's ear and asked, "Who was the second little girl with Nicholas Turner?"

Dexter looked at his wife and shook his head. "Baby, I only saw one little girl. Her name was Karen."

By then, they had reached the front pews of the church. Joey Justice, Misty Wilhite, and Jessica Queen all sat together, smiling broadly at Megan. Megan smiled back almost as exuberantly as the other three.

"Father Cantore!" called Dexter. "Come meet my wife!"

A rotund man in priest's clothing walked over to them, smiling. Father Giuseppe Cantore was balding on top, with hair all around the sides of his head, with graying temples, a blustery red face, and a smile that lit up the church. He opened his arms wide, and took both Dexter and Megan into them, hugging both as if he'd known them all his life.

"It's so *good* to see you, Dexter!" said the priest. "And you have finally married that sweet girl!" To Megan, Father Cantore said, "He used to come talk to me about how much he loved you, Megan. He would tell me little things that you did that endeared you to his heart. Please take good care of my Dexter, and I wish you both a long and happy life!"

Almost before Megan could thank the priest, Father Cantore had moved on to Louie.

"Champ!" shouted the priest. "How are you, my tough friend?"

Louie wrapped the priest in a huge bear hug. The priest was almost hidden by the big man's smiling, enthusiastic hug.

"Excuse me, but could you blokes please spare me the bloody affection?" said a voice with a Cockney London accent from behind them.

Dexter and Megan turned to see who had spoken. Gil Mullins, in person, was standing behind Dexter. Dexter, totally ignoring what Mullins had said, hugged the drummer, then turned to introduce his wife.

"Gil, you British horse's behind, I'd like you to meet my wife. Megan, this is Gil Mullins," said Dexter.

After her mouth had a couple of false starts in speaking, Megan finally stammered, "I-I'm p-pleased to meet you." She held out her hand.

Mullins looked down at her hand, then looked at Dexter. "Megan surely doesn't know us at all, does she?" He looked at Megan, took her outstretched hand, and pulled her to him. "C'mere, you!" He hugged her briefly.

Father Cantore was rushing toward them from the back of the church. "Oh, my...the Christmas mass is in five minutes! Please, take seats! You're in the front two rows! Sit down, sit down, please!"

Megan found herself sitting between Dexter and Gil Mullins. Louie sat on the other side of Mullins.

At midnight, Father Cantore began the Christmas mass.

When it was over, Father Cantore asked Mullins to come forward and speak a few words.

Mullins rose, and approached the altar. Father Cantore directed Mullins to a podium with a microphone. Mullins took his place, with his hands on either side of the podium.

"Merry Christmas, everyone," Mullins began. "Years ago, I had the good fortune to be snowed in here at St. Francis. With me were my good friends, Dexter Beck and Percy Washington...I know, I know...He prefers 'Louie'..." The crowd chuckled, and Mullins laughed, then said into the microphone, "You know, there's a story behind that nickname...I finally heard it tonight from Misty Wilhite. But, that's a story for another time. Tonight, I want to tell you what happened on the night of the Great Christmas Blizzard here in your city..." And he continued with the story.

Mullins' eyes were watery when he got to the part about the Nativity statue of Jesus smiling at him. Megan snuck a quick look at Dexter, and saw that her husband's eyes were quite watery as well. Louie let out a loud sniff, then rubbed his nose as if it itched.

"So, I'd like to end the celebration of the birth of Jesus like I did all those years ago...with a few songs." He started to step away, but came back to the microphone. "Oh, and I'd like my close friends from Justice Security to come down to the railing here, and enjoy the music."

So, the six partners from Justice Security were lined up in front of the altar as Mullins played and sang. Again, as he did that snowy night years ago, he finished with "The Little Drummer Boy".

All eyes in the church were focused on the Nativity scene beside the altar, hoping that history would repeat itself.

Megan was watching the Nativity as well, when she noticed the little girl that called herself "Madeline". Madeline was standing slightly behind the three wise men, next to a statue of an angel. When Madeline saw that Megan had seen her, she held her finger to her mouth again, then pointed to the statue of the baby Jesus.

Megan looked at the statue. It was glowing brightly. Megan gasped, then looked around her. No one else was reacting to the glow. She quickly looked at Madeline again.

Madeline shook her head with her hands over her eyes, then looked into Megan's. Madeline silently mouthed the words, "Be strong", then pointed to the Nativity statue again.

To her surprise, Megan saw that the baby was smiling at her.

Megan quickly looked again toward the spot that Madeline stood, only to see the little girl waving at her as she slowly faded from sight.

Megan, with a deep sense of warmth, smiled to herself on this Christmas Day, and felt blessed. And she *believed*.

THE WRECK OF THE EDMUND FITZGERALD

"I can't believe you talked me into sailing on *this* boat, Jacky," said David Rudolph to his friend, Jacky Baker. "I mean, the owner has some serious guts naming a two-hundred-twenty-foot fishing boat the *Edmund Fitzgerald II.* That's almost daring the sea gods to do their damndest to us."

"I think it lends some prestige to our jobs," replied Jacky. "I've seen some of the men that have sailed her. When they talk to women, they mention that they're on the *Fitzgerald.* Most women have heard the name, but don't realize that the first *Fitzgerald* sailed the Great Lakes...but they sure cozy up to them quickly! That might make sailing with this boat worth it all!"

The two young men walked down the Oregon coast pier toward their new fishing boat. They had both been working as commercial fishermen for seven years, and were well-regarded in the tight-knit fishing community. As good friends since their first sailing assignment, they had chosen to work together...and when the two positions came open on the *Edmund Fitzgerald II,* they jumped at the chance. The owners of the *Fitzgerald II* paid slightly higher shares on their catches, so the competition was intense, but David and Jacky had won out.

The captain of the boat, Dean Binkley, was considered a whiz in finding the best fishing spots in the Pacific. Almost every time he dropped his net, it was hauled into the boat full of commercially viable fish. The *Fitzgerald II* was seldom at sea for more than two weeks before its storage areas were full, and they had to head to shore for a final tally.

Captain Binkley had told the two friends to expect to work hard for their eventual payoff and to work as safely as humanly possible – he didn't want to lose a man to unsafe conditions.

David and Jacky agreed, and handshakes confirmed the deal.

As they approached the boat, David laughed. "The *money* makes it worth it, Jacky, old boy! The women are a very close second."

The first mate, Bobby Allison, asked their names, and checked them off on his clipboard. "You two are the last aboard. We're ready to sail. Let me tell the captain, and then I'll show you where to stow your gear."

"Thanks, sir," answered Jacky.

"Hey, my name's Bobby. Remember that, gentlemen."

David nodded. "We will, as long as you remember that I'm David, and he's Jacky."

"Will do. Follow me, guys!"

The *Edmund Fitzgerald II* sailed all day, and a couple of hours into the night. David judged that they were between two hundred and three hundred miles off shore, well into deep water. When the ship dropped anchor, Captain Binkley called all hands to the mess hall.

Eight men and one woman crammed around the two tables in the small cabin that served as the mess hall. The captain made the tenth member of the crew.

David looked around the table at the rest of the crew. In addition to himself, Jacky, and the first mate, the crew included the ship's cook, who was also the only woman on board. Her name was Deb Smith. The other five members of the crew were Jeff Denniston, Ken Owens, Brent Holland, David Birckhead, and Andy Webb.

As Allison introduced the two new men to the rest of the crew, it was mentioned that Ken Owens, in his late twenties, had just become engaged.

Holland, a crochety old joker from deep in Mississippi, said, in his raspy voice, "Hey, Kenny, if you're gettin' married, I know where you can find you a ring. That is, if you don't mind a brown one."

Owens, playing along, asked, "Where?"

"Crack of my ass."

The crew all laughed heartily at the crude humor, even the cook.

David asked, "So how does a woman handle being not just the cook, and a darn good one, but also being the only woman on board?"

Deb smiled demurely. "My husband was the cook for several years before me, and, when he was lost overboard in an accident with the net, I asked Captain Binkley if I could take over the job. Everything my Greg knew, he learned from me!"

"I'm sorry, ma'am, no offense was intended," said David.

The petite cook looked David in the eye. "And none was taken, my friend."

The first mate threw a thumb toward Webb. "That fellow there...he's as dependable, steady and useful as they come. But he wouldn't say 'crap' if he had a mouthful!"

Allison pointed at Denniston and Birckhead, and said, "Now, *those* two are like Laurel and Hardy...or, maybe, Abbott and Costello. If something screws up on this boat, one of the two of them is behind it...with the other playing cheerleader!"

Both men looked down and snickered. Denniston said, "Heyyy, Abbott!"

The rest of the crew began laughing.

Captain Binkley walked in as the laughter was dying down. "Well, I see that you scurvy tars are making the new men feel at home."

Several of the crew answered with "yes, sir" or "yes, cap'n".

"Great. Now let's get serious for a minute," Binkley said. He unrolled a chart and laid it out on the first table. He had circled their position. Currents were highlighted, and indicated with arrows, showing direction. Several red X's were written in between their position and the pier that had been their departure point.

"Ever since the Fukushima reactor began leaking radioactive water into the Pacific, this ship has been equipped with some of the most sensitive Geiger counters available, certified for use in deep water. The red X's you see on the chart indicate readings of radioactivity far too high for safe fishing. We are approximately three hundred miles from the Oregon coast right now. It's farther out than I'm comfortable with, but the radioactivity is within safe limits here. We'll have to check each catch as well, just to make sure that nothing eaten from our catch makes anyone sick." He looked around the tables. "Questions?"

"How bad is the radioactivity?" asked David.

The captain looked grim. "Bad enough."

Before sunrise the next morning, the net was prepped, and then lowered into the sea. As the ship swung into position, the captain could tell by the wheel that the net had already begun to fill.

That day's catch was huge: halibut, flounder, salmon, even a few squid were captured, processed, and stored in the ice bays.

The men worked without stopping for sixteen straight hours, pulling load after load into the fishing boat. Several dolphins had been netted, and all but one had survived the trip to the surface inside the net. These were patted on their sides and released back into the deep, along with other unwanted catches, like sharks, starfish, and other rare species.

The captain tolerated no cruelty to these unwanted species, and refused to allow them to be killed simply because they had been trapped in the nets.

Even though the sun was close to setting, Captain Binkley decided to drop the net one more time before calling it a day. The men groaned, but with smiles on their faces.

As the net fanned out and filled up behind the boat, David found himself standing beside Jacky.

"Well, Jacky, still think that impressing the ladies is the only reason to stay aboard the boat?"

Jacky laughed. "Man, we got a chunk of change coming to us!"

"Coming about!" said the captain over the speaker.

The boat began a slow turn to its port side, when the stern suddenly dipped deep into the water, and forward motion stopped. A couple of the men, Owens and Holland, almost went over the stern, but were saved by the safety lines that they had attached to harnesses they wore for just such an occasion. The crane holding the net began bowing toward the sea. The engines strained to move forward, and failed. The captain continued trying for a few seconds, and, suddenly, the boat lurched forward, as if it had been released by a huge rubber band. The bow sprang out of the water as the powerful engines spun the propellers almost at full speed. Men and equipment were strewn first aft, then toward the bow, as the boat sprang forward, and slowed to a complete stop. The captain had shut down the engines.

The entire episode had lasted only thirty to forty-five seconds, but had seemed an eternity.

Men were shouting, including David. "What the hell was *that?*" Others were shouting things like, "Did we snag a submarine?" or "Did we get caught on a reef?"

Jacky looked up at the crane. It was quivering back and forth, like an old car antenna that had been bent over and released. He had come to rest beside David, and Jacky nudged his friend. David turned around, and Jacky pointed up. "Look at that, Davey."

David looked up at the shimmering crane. "We snagged the net on something. Wonder what it was?"

Captain Binkley had come outside the wheelhouse, and had seen the crane quivering. He shouted to the men, "Head count! Now!"

Each man on deck sounded off, and Deb Smith had been in the wheelhouse.

"All present and accounted for, Cap'n," said the first mate, Allison. "And no injuries!"

The captain nodded curtly. "Good. Now, let's see what we snagged in that net. Start drawing in that line!"

"Yes, sir," chorused a couple of the men.

The huge winch started pulling in the line, or steel cable, that held the net. As the net neared the surface, David noticed that the sun had been below the horizon for five minutes or so. The boat's lights didn't provide as much light toward the net as he'd like, but maybe the hands that had been with the boat for a while were used to it, and could see.

The net broke the surface. Birckhead, on the stern with Denniston, shouted, "Net's up, Captain!"

Denniston said, "Wow! Look at that!" He was pointing at the net as it rose higher.

In the poor light, David and Jacky could see that nothing was in the net but a couple of hagfish. The net itself was torn from the topmost part all the way down the side.

"Bring it aboard!" said Allison.

The crane was being prepped to start its turn to bring the net aboard when a huge, fifty foot geyser of water roiled up under the net, and the net disappeared under the surface. The resulting wave splashed over the stern, soaking Birckhead and Denniston. The line attached to the net began screeching through the winch as the slack was being taken up. The crane bowed over again. David, Jacky, and Holland were close to the winch, and Jacky couldn't believe his eyes – the winch was bolted to the deck, and the thick, two-inch boards holding the bolts were bending upwards, toward the stern.

Allison began shouting. "Bolt cutters! Now! Bolt cutters! Cut the line!"

It took a moment before it dawned on David that Allison was shouting in his and Jacky's direction. David leapt up and asked Holland, "Where?"

Holland pointed to the locker beside the deck hatch leading below. David ran to the locker, threw it open, and found the biggest set of bolt cutters he had ever seen.

"Jacky! Get over here!" shouted David. "I can't work these alone! They're too big!"

The stern of the boat began bouncing up and down in the water. The crane seemed to have bowed over as far as it could go. The line holding the net was so tight, if a man could strum it like a guitar string, it would make music. Jacky worked his way to the locker and helped David lift the bolt cutters. As they began making their way toward the winch, water began sloshing over the stern and the sides. Suddenly, they all heard a loud, high-pitched sound.

David wondered what could be making the noise, when Holland shouted, "Look out! Line's about to go!"

His words turned out to be prophetic. Under the surface of the water, the line suddenly snapped. With the tension released, the crane snapped back into place...and whipped the line backwards. The end of the line sprang back with a deafening whip-crack, and smashed into the wheelhouse.

Captain Binkley had stepped out of the wheelhouse, which was mounted on top of the bridge of the boat. He was standing too close to the line as it whipped downward, and had his right arm neatly severed in mid-bicep, as he pointed to something over the side. The line crushed the wheelhouse, and landed directly on Deb Smith. The poor cook was flattened as if she had been hit with a flyswatter, and was dead before she knew what had happened. Both sides of the wheelhouse collapsed when the middle was disintegrated by the downward force of the steel line.

The line, still being whip-cracked by the metal crane, followed its return path, and smacked the water behind the boat. The water absorbed much of the tension remaining in the line, so that the line went slack as it came out of the water. It then hung limply from the end of the crane.

As the *Fitzgerald II* slowly settled from its bouncing, David and Jacky registered that Holland was calling for help.

"Help! Need help! Cap'n Binkley's hurt! Help!"

Being the closest to what was left of the wheelhouse, the two men scrambled up the ladder to the roof of the bridge. Holland was kneeling beside the captain's right side, holding a belt as tight as he could around the severed end of the captain's arm. A pool of blood surrounded both men. Holland's eyes looked haunted as he looked up at David.

"I've done for him as well I can, but he's still bleedin'," he said tonelessly. "He ain't dead yet, but Death's hoverin' about, waiting to touch him."

The captain was a strong man, and was still conscious. His eyes fastened first on David's, then Jacky's. "It was *huge,* I tell you! And its eyes – they *glowed!* It was a monster from Hell, and our time's *up!*"

David had some experience with medical emergencies. Before becoming a fisherman, he had served a tour in the Army, as a medic – it was one of the reasons that Captain Binkley hired them. He went to Holland's side.

"Here, Brent, let me take over. Captain, we have no intention of losing you. Okay, Brent, is there any morphine on board? Any strong pain killers?" David asked.

Holland nodded. "Aye, there's morphine in the first aid locker below." The other men had arrived, one by one.

"Then go *get* it, man, we're gonna need it." David looked at the first mate. "Bobby, until the captain recovers from this, you're in charge. First order of business is to radio for help, and head to shore. The captain needs medical attention now!"

Allison replied, "I'll get us underway within five minutes." He looked around, then pointed at Denniston and Birckhead. "You two! Go below and check the hull of this tub! Make sure that the water we took aboard isn't causing problems. Webb, go secure that damn line. It's caused enough harm." Allison took a deep breath. "Owens, get a plastic tarp and gather what you can of Deb, and put it in the ice. Take Baker with you."

"Sir, I need Baker."

Allison looked down, then nodded his assent. "Keep him for now, then. And, David?"

Rudolph looked up. "Yes, sir?"

"Save the captain if you can."

David nodded grimly.

Allison climbed down the ladder and entered the bridge.

"What do you need me to do, Davey?" asked Jacky.

David took a breath. "Find me a blowtorch, Jacky. We're going to have to cauterize this arm, or the captain will bleed to death."

Jacky gulped. "Okay, David. On my way." He stood, and looked toward the stern. "Where's Webb?"

"Not now, Jacky, we need that torch!"

Jacky slid down the ladder and was gone.

David, holding the tourniquet tightly, spoke quietly to the captain. "Dean, I won't lie. This is gonna hurt like you have never hurt before – even with the morphine."

Binkley opened his eyes and found David's. "Doesn't matter, David. You didn't *see* that thing! It's huge! Its eyes glowed *red,* and spread from..."

"I got the kit, David," interrupted Holland. "But we got more problems. I gotta tell Allison – seawater is covering half the engines." He handed David the first aid kit, then went back down the ladder.

"We're dead, then," said Binkley quietly, closing his eyes. "The *Fitzgerald II* is a good ship and true, but she's just a cork in the water compared to that thing."

David felt a chill run down his spine as he used one hand to pat the captain's arm. "We'll be all right, Captain. There's still the radio."

"No, there isn't," said Allison from behind David. "When the line wrecked the wheelhouse, the coaxial cable for the antenna wrapped around it, and, since both radios, bridge *and* wheelhouse, were attached to it, they were both whipped into the sea. And we're too far out to have cell phone service."

"How about a satellite phone?" asked David.

"Owner bought the Geiger counters instead."

David was quiet for a few seconds. "Bobby, will you help me with a morphine dose? I need to get him as loopy as possible before I cauterize that arm. And I can only use one hand."

"Doesn't matter now, David."

"Why?"

"Captain Binkley's dead. Take a look."

David looked. Binkley had stopped breathing. His skin was pale, almost white, from the blood loss. David relaxed his grip on the makeshift tourniquet.

"Damn. He was a good man, and a good captain," said David.

Allison wiped a tear. "You don't know the half of it, David."

"So, what do we do now, Bobby?"

Allison studied the deck for a moment. "We'll pump the water out of the engine room, and see how bad the seawater hurt them. If they're shot, I guess we could rig some kind of sail..."

Allison was interrupted by Jacky's return. In his hand, he had a propane blowtorch. "Will this do, Davey?" he asked, out of breath.

"It's too late, Jacky," replied David. "He slipped away while you were gone. Too much blood loss."

"Aw, *man!*" replied Jacky. He was quiet for a moment, then turned to Allison. "I almost forgot! No one can find Webb. He's not on the stern, and he's not below. Birckhead and Denniston are looking below, but it's almost a wasted effort. He's gone."

Allison swore bitterly and threw his hat down onto the deck. "Then where the hell is he?"

After a few seconds, David said, "Maybe he was taken by whatever took the net."

"What do you mean 'took the net'?" asked Allison.

"Something took the net like it was bait on a hook, and bounced this boat like a bobber on a fishing pole," David replied. He pointed to the captain. "*He* saw it, whatever it was. He said its eyes glowed red...and something about it being huge!"

"Nothing but ravings of a dying man! We snagged the net on something – a reef, an outcropping of underwater rocks! Nothing alive is big enough to bounce a two hundred foot boat! Not even a humpback!"

"Unless it's something that's mutated," said Jacky quietly.

David looked at the deck. Personally, he was thinking the same thing.

Allison looked like he'd just bit into a lemon. "*Mutated?* Have you lost your senses, man?"

David shook his head. "No, not really. There are news reports from everywhere that deep water species have been coming to the surface with some regularity, like giant squid and big great whites. Who knows what is down there, and how it will be affected by the radioactive water leak? It's been leaking long enough for a couple of generations of most species down there...one of them could have mutated in a way that no one was expecting. Even the captain wanted to check each fish for radioactivity."

"You sound like a damn Godzilla movie," said Allison. "Secure that, now. I'll hear no more of it." He looked at each man. "Since we're short a cook, I hope you two can throw together some kind of meal. We're going to need it. See to it."

David and Jacky chorused, "Yes, sir."

Allison climbed down to the main deck and entered the bridge.

Ken Owens had been within earshot of the whole exchange as he retrieved what was left of Deb Smith's body. He approached the two men quietly.

"Guys," he said quietly. "Do you really believe what you just said?"

David looked at Owens. "I have chills and goose bumps right now. Live or die, this is my last sea voyage."

Jacky nodded agreement.

The two men did indeed have galley experience. They produced a meal that was tasty and filling.

It was only a meal for seven, however. Webb had not been found anywhere on the boat, and the Captain and Smith were dead.

"Brent, how do the engines look?" asked Allison.

Holland swallowed. "Well, the water pumped out easy, and I cleaned and oiled all the parts that were under water. I replaced the plugs and points, and none of the seals leaked water into the delicate stuff. I'd say they're worthy, if the fuel ain't contaminated." He dipped his yeast roll into his beef stew and took another bite. "Generator's working fine, though," he said around his food. "It's set above the deck, and the water never got to her."

"Good news there, then," replied Allison. "All right, men, let's try to get some shuteye as soon as supper is secured. We'll try the engines at first light, and see if we can get out of here."

Sleep was a long time coming, however. The six men shared a good-sized cabin. Eight bunks were lined along the walls, four to each side. Allison had his own small cabin.

Owens, of course, had spread the word about the speculation of a mutated predator, and discussion was quite enthusiastic about what kind of creature might have mutated to such a dangerous size. The problem was that no one had seen anything except the captain...but the circumstantial evidence pointed to something big.

As the night drew on, and the exhausted men wore down, one by one, they drifted off to sleep. Finally, all was mostly silent, with the exception of a few snores.

WHAM!

Five of the men were knocked from their bunks. David only held his place because he had long ago learned to tie a couple of lines across his bunk to keep from being tossed out of it during rough seas. All of the men were shouting and scrambling around until, finally, one of them located a light and switched it on.

They found clothes and threw them on. As each man dressed as much as he could, he ran out of the cabin door and up onto the deck.

Allison was already there.

"What was that, Bobby?" asked Owens.

Allison, with a slight trembling in his voice, said, "I...I don't know."

David said, "It felt like something hit the boat...or the boat hit something."

"Boat's not moving," said Jacky, and immediately wished he hadn't.

Allison's face reddened. "I thought I told you men to secure that sh..."

WHAM!

The hit spun the boat 45 degrees to port, and knocked all of the men to the deck. Water splashed up onto the deck from the starboard side, but rolled off of the deck through the drains. The men had secured all hatches leading below. They didn't want to risk the engines again.

Birckhead was the first to his feet. He looked out to the stern. "Um, guys, I'm not stoned, so what is that?" He pointed.

The rest of the men climbed rapidly to their feet and looked in the direction Birckhead indicated.

Two huge, red, glowing orbs were heading directly toward the *Fitzgerald II* at a seemingly lazy pace.

Into the men's silence, David said quietly, "Oh, my dear God."

Jacky said to Allison, "Looks like we're all seeing your 'dying man's ravings', Allison."

Owens said, "Gentlemen, I believe it might be a good idea to brace ourselves. Whatever that thing is, it's about to hit us again."

That broke their paralysis. Each man scrambled to tie themselves to something sturdy before they were hit.

"Oh, man," said Holland, still staring off the stern. "That thing's eyes are staring *forward!* They aren't on either side of its head! It's looking forward! It's a predator for sure! And it's way bigger than any..."

WHAM!

The boat had been hit dead astern, and hard enough to knock it up out of the water, where it sailed effortlessly through the air for twenty feet. The boat landed again with a splash. With the initial bump, the anchor chain snapped, and the boat floated freely.

Brent Holland had not taken the time to secure himself, and when the boat was hit, he was knocked astern, but still on the boat. When the boat landed, Holland was bounced off of the stern into the sea.

Holland was a strong swimmer, and began swimming toward the boat. With no anchor to slow it, the boat was still moving along the surface at several knots per hour. It was slowing, but it was further away than Holland liked. He began shouting.

"Kenny! Allison! Ahoy, the boat! Need help! I'm in the water! I'm here!" He waved his arms in the moonlit night, hoping that he could be seen.

On the boat, Denniston had been tossed like a rag doll when the slack in his line gave way. His neck had been broken when he landed on one of the storage lockers on the deck, and his glassy eyes stared to the stern as if he were looking for Holland...or, perhaps, waiting for him.

David, Jacky, and Birckhead had all gotten into the safety harnesses that were lined along the port side of the rear of the boat. Allison was still in his harness, but the slack in his line had given way, and he was dangling over the side of the boat. Owens had been bounced a bit, but remained unharmed. He gained his feet first, and turned one of the spotlights toward the sound of Holland's voice. After a bit of swinging about, the light had pinpointed the man waving his arm at them from the water. Holland looked to be four to five hundred feet behind the boat.

"Hang on, Brent!" shouted Owens. "We'll get you in a minute!"

"Well, hurry *up*, dammit! I really don't wanna be in the wat..."

Bloop

The sound of a pebble dropping into water...quiet, calm...and Holland was gone.

Jacky, Birckhead, and David had all scrambled out of the harnesses. David was looking at the sea all around the boat, trying to spot the glowing orbs before they were taken by surprise.

From the starboard side of the boat, a quiet voice was heard. "Would you gentlemen please pull me back into the boat? I really feel like bait on a hook right now."

Allison. Birckhead and Jacky moved to pull the first mate out of the water, but when the line cleared the side, it had been cleanly cut. Allison was gone.

David, meanwhile, had had enough. "Guys, I say let's abandon ship. Whatever that is, this boat fascinates it, and I don't want to be here when it gets around to taking a chunk out of it!"

The other three men agreed.

The *Edmund Fitzgerald II* was equipped with two boats suitable for use as lifeboats, and as runabouts between boats, or the *Fitzgerald II* and the shore. They were fifteen feet long, and had very powerful outboard motors on the back. Each runabout had two ten gallon cans of fuel, along with a supply of food and water aboard...and walkie-talkies for communicating back and forth.

The four men decided to take both boats, with David and Jacky in one boat, Owens and Birckhead in the other. They all retrieved a few personal belongings from below, then each pair climbed into the boats. The boats were then lowered into the water.

David took the walkie-talkie, and spoke into it. "Kenny, Jim, do you copy?"

"We do," came Birckhead's response.

"Let's head due east...we're bound to hit land sometime."

"Copy that."

Both outboards had electric starters, so no pulling of ropes was required. Both motors started right up, and both boats met under the bow of the *Fitzgerald II.* Jacky was manning one motor and Owens the other. As they pulled side by side, David yelled to Birckhead.

"East is that way!" he said, and pointed with his hand.

Birckhead nodded, then turned pale. He pointed to the port side of his runabout. "Look!"

All four men turned. The glowing, red orbs were heading for the *Fitzgerald II* at another leisurely pace.

"Time to go, boys!" said David.

Jacky and Owens fired up their outboards, and both boats sped to the east. To port and a bit astern, the orbs began getting smaller as they came closer.

David's radio squawked, then Birckhead's voice was heard. "Where'd it go? Didja see where it went?"

"No, I didn't. If I had to guess, I'd say it went deep," replied David.

All four men heard a huge splash behind them. They turned, and saw a sight that none of them would ever forget.

The thing had leaped from the sea behind them. It made the two-hundred-twenty-foot *Edmund Fitzgerald II* look like a toy floating in a bathtub. The moon shed very little light on the monster, but the men could see that it had a broad, flat face, with forward facing eyes. That was all the detail that they could see...or *wanted* to see.

The creature turned in the air, and came down on the *Fitzgerald II*. Its hideously large mouth was open, and the fishing boat was swallowed as the creature fell back into the sea. A huge swell began rippling out in all directions from the place the creature dove, and overtook the two boats quickly.

Since the swell came from the stern, riding it out was not going to be easy. The men did not have time to turn the boats, and the swell was at least twenty-five feet tall. Jacky fought the swell with the outboard, and finally hit the top, and began going down the back. Owens was not as experienced with the small motor, however. The small boat capsized as David and Jacky's boat hit normal seas again. Birckhead was thrown from the boat into the air, and landed five feet from David and Jacky. He was quickly pulled into the boat.

They never saw Owens, or his runabout, again.

"Wow," said Birckhead. "Think we'll make it back to shore?"

David looked grim. "I hope so. Somebody's got to notify the authorities about that thing."

Jacky said, "Know what scares me about that thing?"

"What's that?" asked David.

"If there's one, there's bound to be more. I'd hate to think about what the Pacific will be like with those things swimming around."

Locked in their thoughts, the men rode quietly as the boat sped into the rising sun.

GOLD

B ecky Patterson was getting dressed. She had just gotten out of the shower, and was getting ready to meet her friend, Pam Snyder. Both girls were from Redding, California, and they planned to go to out to Whiskeytown Lake for the weekend.

Pam had met some guy at the bar that employed her. He played guitar, and he was going to Whiskeytown this weekend, too, but separately. Pam had the hots for the guy, but she wasn't sure enough about the man to go alone. Pam had learned a couple of hard lessons while working at the bar. So, Becky was tagging along, too, as moral support and a way to bail out if necessary.

Becky and Pam had been best friends since fifth grade, and still were. Both women were blonde, and both were very attractive. After high school, neither girl's family could afford to send them to college, so they went to work. At first, both were working for a grocery store chain. When Pam turned twenty-one, she went to work for the bar as a waitress. She made good money, often bringing home more money than Becky during certain weeks. Tips were good, but Becky had just made cashier manager, which included a raise along with the responsibility. The girls had been roommates since about six months after they had started working, and their friendship had remained solid.

Now twenty-two, both young women were wondering if there was more to life than work and going out every weekend.

Pam crashed through the front door, in a hurry as always. "Becky! Beck-eee! Are you ready yet? We have to get there before nightfall, so we can see how to put up the tent!"

"Almost done, Pam, hold on," replied Becky. *I'll enjoy the trip to the lake,* she thought, *but I don't want to be a fifth wheel. So, I want to go, and I don't. Go figure.* "Is the car all loaded, Pamdunk?" Becky asked, using Pam's old high school nickname.

"All is loaded except for your suitcase, Becky-the-deck," said Pam.

Both women began giggling.

When the laughing slowed down, Becky began putting on her makeup. "I'm not feeling a hundred percent about this trip, Pam."

Pam stood in the bathroom doorway, looking at Becky's reflection. "Why, Becky?"

Becky shook her head. "I don't know. It's nothing I can put my finger on."

"Should we just stay home this weekend? Maybe catch a movie?" asked Pam.

Becky actually considered this for a moment. "No, we'll go. Maybe that feeling will go away later."

"You sure, Becky?"

Becky nodded. "Sure. I don't want to be the death of a possible relationship!" She shivered. *Goose walked over my grave.*

True to Northern Califonia cliches, the car they were taking was a late-model Volkswagen Beetle convertible. It was Becky's, although both girls used it. It had a special rack on the back that allowed the girls to bring their bicycles. The back seat was piled high with a tent, camping gear, food, a camp stove, a cooler filled with ice and cold food, and suitcases.

The ride to Whiskeytown Lake was pleasant. The late Friday afternoon sun was slanted just right, the temperature was nice, and the girls talked and laughed during the trip.

"So what's this guitar player's name?" asked Becky.

"Jeff Madden," replied Pam.

"Where's he from?"

Pam shrugged. "I don't know. The conversation didn't get that far. His last gig was over, he was packing up, and the bar was closing. He invited me to go to the lake with him, and I said I could meet him there, and that my roommate and best friend would be coming with me. Then," she said breathlessly, as she grasped Becky's arm, "he smiled at me with the biggest, most charming smile I've ever seen!" She giggled. "It's like I was instantly aroused! I've never seen a smile like it!"

Becky grinned. "Pam, a stiff *breeze* makes you aroused! It always has!"

Both women began laughing again.

When the women arrived at the park, they chose to set up camp at Horse Camp. Once there, it was getting dark, and they were hungry. Rather than eat first, Pam convinced Becky that they should find Jeff first, and invite him to eat with them.

They found Jeff rather quickly at the Brandy Creek picnic area. He was seated at one of the picnic tables, and had a blazing fire going in one of the fire grills. The guitar player was idly strumming the instrument, not playing anything in particular.

"Jeff!" called Pam, as she stood on her tiptoes and waved.

Jeff turned, saw the women, and waved, with a huge smile on his face. He stood and faced them, and Becky saw why Pam was so excited about him. The man was very good-looking, about six feet tall, with light brown hair, a neatly trimmed beard, and a thin physique. But the thin appearance hid wiry muscles, and he projected a sense of strength. His eyes were a light blue, the lightest blue she had ever seen. His smile revealed even, white teeth.

Wow! I see why Pam likes him! He make me *a little aroused, too!*

"Jeff, I'd like you to meet my roommate and best friend, Becky Patterson," said Pam.

Jeff turned his hundred-watt smile to Becky, and held out his hand. "Nice to meet you! My name's Jeff Madden."

Becky took his hand, and felt a small tingle at the base of her spine. "Nice to meet you, too. Pam's spoken of you quite a bit."

"Drove her crazy, is what she means to say," said Pam.

Jeff threw his head back and laughed heartily. So did both women.

"Well, I've certainly thought quite a bit about you, too," Jeff said to Pam.

Pam smiled demurely. "Thank you. Listen, we were going to throw together some dinner...nothing fancy, of course. Would you like to join us?"

"Could we eat it here?" asked Jeff. "It's so beautiful here."

Pam looked at Becky, who shrugged.

"We'd have to go back to the campsite and get the food, but I don't see a problem with it," said Becky.

"Want to walk with us?" asked Pam.

"I would, but my campsite is back there," said Jeff, gesturing vaguely behind him. "I haven't pitched the tent yet, or anything else. Do you mind if I wait here?"

"Not a bit. We'll be back in a little while," answered Pam.

Later, after the sun had gone down, the trio sat in camp chairs around the fire grill. Night sounds were all around them – crickets and night birds, mostly. Dinner had been consumed, and the three were talking, while Jeff strummed odd notes on his guitar. Nothing he strummed could be construed as a song, or even a piece of a song.

Pam asked, "Jeff, since your gig ended at the bar, what are you going to do now?"

Jeff looked up. "I really don't know. I had hoped that the bar scene would last longer than it did, but, that's the way these things happen. I know one thing: I need something pretty quick, because it sure didn't pay enough to keep me for long!"

Here comes the pitch, thought Becky.

"I don't see that Becky or I would be able to help you financially, Jeff," said Pam.

Go, Pam! You've learned something from those deadbeats you used to date!

"California girls are the greatest in the world, but I don't expect either of you to fork over any money. I'd never dream of asking." Jeff sounded a little bit offended.

Pam hurried to take the sting from her words. "I'm sorry, Jeff. I've met a few guys that looked at me as money in the bank, instead of a girlfriend. So has Becky."

Jeff laughed cynically. "I guess you have. Too many guys look at women as objects, or extra money, or maids. They don't realize what women are."

Becky couldn't resist. "What's that, Jeff?"

Jeff stopped strumming the guitar and looked at her. "They're works of art, Becky. Songs in the making. I guess, as a musician, that's how I look at them. I mean, I *know* they're people, too, with real feelings. But, I can hear their melodies, and I can play them. And, like me, there are people that can turn music into gold."

Becky snorted. "Sounds like you're bragging."

Pam glared at Becky. "Becky! Be polite!"

"I'm sorry, Pam, but this just seems like another line to me! No offense, Jeff, but we hear stuff like this all the time! Guys just seem to make it up as they go along. Anything to get into our pants!"

"Becky! *Really?*" said Pam.

Jeff held up a hand. "Pam, it's okay! I understand Becky's skepticism. I guess I'll have to show you." He looked at Becky, and his eyes seemed to have a golden glow.

Reflection from the fire, she thought. But she still had goosebumps!

Jeff glanced around, as if to make sure that they were alone. "Your stories are there for the taking. I'll play Pam's melody first. One requirement from both of you, however: close your eyes and give yourself to the music."

"Sounds pretty corny," said Becky.

"Oh, come on, Becky, what's it gonna hurt?" said Pam.

"Oh, all right," agreed Becky.

Both women closed their eyes.

As the first note drifted across the picnic area, the night went silent. The melody coming from Jeff's guitar was both relaxing and exciting, and the young women began smiling. They started to slowly rock side to side in time with the music.

To Becky, it seemed as if the music was alive. It was both beautiful and haunting. It felt as if the music had always been, and always would be. She wondered if she had been hypnotized by it, and found that she didn't really care.

Becky assumed she was dreaming. She tried opening her eyes, and, dreamlike, she could see the golden and melodic notes and bars that made up the music. She watched them wrap themselves around Pam, and she thought they were swirling faster and faster, circling her friend. Becky knew she was dreaming, however, because it seemed as if Pam turned a bright, golden color...and shrank as the notes whirled around her. A quick, dreamlike glance at Jeff revealed that not only had his eyes began glowing gold, but a golden aura had surrounded him as he strummed the melody from the stringed instrument. His smile had widened almost halfway around his head, and it seemed that his teeth had grown longer. Still convinced that she was dreaming, she glanced at Pam just in time to see her transform into a golden coin sitting in the center of the camp chair.

Becky closed her eyes again, and they remained closed until she could no longer hear the music. She opened them briefly and saw that Pam was not there.

Wrinkling her brow, still under the effects of the music, she asked, "Where's Pam?"

Jeff gestured somewhere behind him. "Bathroom. Ready for your song?"

Becky nodded, and the music began playing. She could feel it swirling all around her as she closed her eyes and lost herself in the hypnotic melody.

The *Cash For Gold!* store in Redding, California, opened promptly at nine AM on Saturday. The store was operated by two partners, Jimmy Grimes and Charlie Wills. They bought scrap and unwanted gold, melted it down and sold the ingots to jewelry stores, private minting firms, and, occasionally, the U. S. government, for use in making its gold bullion coins.

Jimmy Grimes was working the front counter that Saturday, while Charlie operated the smelter in the back room. They had purchased several ounces of gold, and were melting down what they had bought during the week. Grimes had barely gotten back behind the counter after unlocking the front door, when a customer entered.

Grimes smiled at the tall man with the beard and the blue eyes. "Morning! What can I do for you today?"

The man dug into his pocket as he spoke. "Got a couple of gold coins to get rid of. I need some cash – the rent's due." The man pulled out two good-sized coins.

"I hear *that*," said Grimes. "I'll have to run a couple of tests on these. Is that okay? I ask, because it might damage them a little."

"That's fine."

Grimes ran his tests. The coins were pure, twenty-four karat gold. He weighed them – just a bit over three ounces. He went back to the customer, and named an offer.

The customer nodded. "I'll take it."

Grimes looked at the front of the coins. Highly detailed imprints of women were on both coins, in profile...they looked sort of familiar.

"Um, could I have that in cash, please?" asked the customer, pulling Grimes from his reverie.

"Sure, I just need you to fill out these forms, please," replied Grimes.

The man filled out all of the required forms, and showed a photo ID. Grimes counted out the cash, and said, "Thank you, sir. If you have any other private mint coins like these, please bring them to us. We'll pay you top dollar, Mister...," he glanced down at the paperwork, "Madden," he finished.

"Will do," said the customer, as he left the store.

Grimes picked up the coins. He glanced down at them as he walked toward the back. The portraits on the coins, face-on to the front of each coin, still made him think of someone he'd seen before.

Wait a minute, thought Grimes. *Weren't these in profile before?*

Puzzled, he took them to his partner.

"Charlie, take a look at these," said Grimes. "Do the women on the front look familiar?" He held the coins up for Wills to see, since Wills needed both hands for the hot work.

Wills peered at the coins, then shook his head. "Nobody that I recognize," he said. "Hey, how pure are those?"

"Twenty-four Karat," replied Grimes.

"Hey, just in time! Throw them in the pot – that's what I'm melting down right now!"

Grimes took one last look at the coins. The women pictured on both coins had their fists up, as if they were pounding on a window...

Creeped out, Grimes tossed the coins into the melting pot, and watched as they became liquid along with the other gold.

HOT CHILD IN THE CITY

"I really don't know, Johnny," said Detective Third Grade James William Coleman. Some of the other detectives on the force referred to him as "Jim Bill"...it was sort of a tribute both to Coleman's southern heritage, and to the old TV show, *The Waltons*. He was okay with that. It made him feel special. Of course, Jim Bill *was* special. He had only been on the police force for five years. He signed up directly out of college with a Criminal Justice degree, and had made Detective Third in only four years. He was twenty-seven years old.

His partner, Detective First Grade John Yates, was seated in a booth across from Jim Bill. They were in a small club in Bohemian Village in this city, and were assigned to the "Dance Murders". Four people had been murdered in the Village, and all of them had been mutilated and dismembered horribly. The heart and liver from each victim had been taken, and it was assumed that the killer was taking trophies from each murder. The fact of the missing organs had not been shared with the press, so that the police force had something to help weed out fake confessions.

Each victim had been seen dancing in one of the Village's nightclubs before they were murdered. All were male.

"Don't know what, Jim Bill?" asked Yates, between swallows from his beer.

Coleman took a swallow from his own beer. "I don't know if this is a good idea or not, staking out a couple of night clubs every night." He gestured to the two of them. "I mean, *look* at us! Even when we dress down to fit in, we still scream 'cop'!"

"Hey, it's what the captain wanted, right?" said Yates. "So we're here." He drank more beer.

"Yeah, I guess so," said Coleman. He laughed. "A couple of more years, and we'll be too old to stake out clubs!"

Yates laughed, too. Yates was thirty. When Yates stopped laughing, he lifted his beer to take a drink. As he lifted, he shifted his eyes to the dance floor. His eyes widened, and his hand froze in motion.

Coleman looked up and noticed his partner. "What's got you?" He turned to look in the direction that Yates was staring.

At first, Coleman didn't see anything. Then he did. His mouth slowly dropped open, and his eyes widened.

The girl was dressed in black. A black tank top with spaghetti straps, black short shorts, and black sneakers with no socks. Her hair was either really dark brown, or black, her makeup was minimal, and her legs were long, shapely, and just the right amount of tan. Her eyes were a dark brown, and her eyelashes were longer than most. Her body, hinted at under the shorts and top, appeared to be just right.

She was dancing. It didn't appear that she was dancing *with* anyone, but, nowadays, the two detectives just couldn't tell.

She was the most beautiful girl Coleman or Yates had ever seen.

Finally, the girl took a break, and disappeared from sight, and both men moved.

"Oh, my God," said Yates quietly. "Did you *see* her?"

Coleman was just as starstruck as Yates. He nodded. "I did. I thought my tongue was going to hit the floor!"

Just then, the waitress came to their table. "You guys want anything else?"

"Yeah, I do," said Yates. "Jim Bill? I'm buying."

"Sure, I'll take a beer," replied Coleman. "Say, can you help us out?" he asked the waitress. He showed her his badge. Sometimes it greased the skids a little.

The waitress smiled. "Sure. Whatcha wanna know?"

Coleman grinned sheepishly. "I'd like to know that girl's name – the one dressed in black."

The waitress laughed out loud. "Yeah, you and every other male in the place! Nobody knows her name, or where she came from, or anything else about her. Every guy in here," she waved her hand around the room, "wants to take her home." She leaned closer to the two men. "*I* think she's hungry...and kinda dangerous!" She stood up. "I'll be back with your beers in just a minute."

Yates looked at Coleman. "You horn dog!"

Coleman shrugged and grinned. "Hey, I'm single, Johnny. What can I say?"

Yates laughed. "And she's probably jailbait, buddy-boy!"

"Nah...I bet she's eighteen...but not much older."

"And that still makes her awfully young, Jim Bill."

"You forget – I'm only twenty-seven," said Coleman. He pointed a finger at his partner. "And *you* are married!"

The waitress appeared with their beers, and placed one in front of each detective. Yates paid for the drinks, and gave the waitress a generous tip.

"Wow! Thanks!" she said. She leaned closer to the two men, and said, "She's on the dance floor again, if you were looking for her." She stood up. "Just trying to help! Have a great night, guys!" She waved and headed back toward the bar.

Yates looked at his partner's sheepish smile and said, "Well, far be it from me to stand in the way of romance. I'll drink this and head home, so you can go chase your hot child." He picked up his beer and drank several swallows, then put it down decisively on the table in front of him.

"I'm gone, Jim Bill. Tonight's stakeout has been a big zero." Yates stood, then leaned close to Coleman. "Be safe, partner. See you tomorrow."

"You too, Johnny," replied Coleman. "Take care."

Yates waved as he turned and left the club.

Coleman watched his partner go, then drank a few swallows of beer. *The heck with it!* he thought to himself. *Might as well give it a shot! If I ask, all she can do is say no.*

Coleman got up and maneuvered to the other side of the dance floor, bobbing and dodging through the crowd like a pro boxer. The detective made it to the other side of the dance floor, and couldn't find the girl. He actually felt a tiny sliver of panic in the pit of his stomach when he couldn't find her – *how could she have gotten away?* Then, someone tapped him on the shoulder. He turned to see who had tapped him.

It was the girl.

Coleman's eyes widened. Her beauty was even more powerful up close. The girl's eyes were like deep, brown orbs of light that captured a man's spirit and left him feeling as if nothing else existed, and nothing else mattered, except losing one's self in them. Her hair was like deep brown silken threads, smooth and shining, catching the light and reflecting it. He felt lost...no, mesmerized... and knew this one thing: he had to be the man in this girl's life, forever.

"Hi," she said. "I hear that you've been looking for me." She smiled gently.

Coleman nodded slowly, still caught up in the trance.

"Here I am," she said.

Coleman stretched his arms out as if to take the girl into them and hold her tight. She placed a hand firmly on his chest...*She touched me! She actually touched me!*...and pushed him back.

"Not yet," she said with a smile.

Coleman asked her a question, forcing the words out. "Are...you from...around here? I mean, are you from the city?"

The girl just smiled at him.

"What's your name?" he asked.

She opened her mouth to tell him...and his cell phone chose that moment to ring. A very quick look of annoyance crossed her face – too quickly for anyone to notice – and the smile was back. "Your phone is ringing."

Coleman, who knew that the noise he was hearing was something he should pay attention to, said, "Oh!" He shook his head as if to clear it, then took his phone out of his pocket.

Yates was calling.

Coleman looked at the girl, and said, "It's my partner. I have to answer it."

She nodded, and he turned away to answer.

"Hey, Johnny, baaaad timing! What's wrong?"

"You ain't gonna believe this," said Yates. "Somebody stole my damn car!"

"You gotta be kidding!"

"Nope. There's glass all over the street right beside the space I parked in. Damn thief just broke the glass and hot-wired it, I guess...but it's sure as hell gone. Will you please come give me a ride home?"

Coleman hesitated, then said, "Sure, Johnny. Where'd you park?"

Yates told him, and Coleman hung up. He turned to tell the girl that he had to leave, but she had disappeared.

The next morning, the captain called the whole squad into the conference room. Another murder had occurred the night before, and the victim had been seen dancing in the very club that Yates and Coleman had been assigned to.

"You two want to tell me if you were on stakeout, or were you cruising for a little fun on the side?" asked the captain.

Coleman opened his mouth to say something, but Yates beat him to it.

"Captain, we were there. We watched everybody. Nobody came in that looked suspicious. You know how hard it is to pick out a crazy like this perp? It's darn near impossible! Unless he comes in with a bleeding machete or something, we're not going to know who it is! All we can do is maybe follow them when they leave, and try to stop it while it's going on."

The captain thought for a minute. "That's not a bad idea. That's what you need to do, is follow the ones that leave alone. The ones that leave in groups, you don't have to worry about...it's the people that leave alone. When they do, you follow them."

Awwww, crap! thought Coleman.

The two detectives kept watch on everyone. Although he was watching everyone, and doing his job, Coleman watched *for* only one person, and wondered if she'd come back.

The men decided to take turns following each male that left the club, just to make sure they got home safely. So far, Yates had broken up two fistfights, and Coleman had stopped a mugging, arresting the mugger and sending him to jail with a patrol car. The victim rode in a separate patrol car in order to press charges, and Coleman instructed the patrolmen to make sure that the victim was driven home safely.

As Coleman was walking back to the club, his head came up suddenly, as if he had caught a whiff of the girl's scent. He looked around wildly, trying to locate her, and then he saw her.

She was across the street, ahead of him, passing under a streetlight. Coleman began following her from his side of the street, watching her walk. It was a dark night, and a not-safe part of town, but she walked like she just didn't care. Briskly she walked, but not in a hurry, hips swaying slightly, arms swinging in sync with the opposite leg. Men she passed on the sidewalk all stopped to stare. He couldn't believe that she would be brave enough to walk through this part of town...but, it was obvious that she was heading toward the club he and Yates were staking out.

Coleman was elated. He just *knew* that he was the right man for this girl!

The club came into sight on her side of the street, so Coleman crossed over the busy intersection. By the time he crossed, she had disappeared inside. When he got inside, the first person he saw was Yates.

"Your girl is here," he said with a smile. "Looking as beautiful as ever!"

"I know she's here. I followed her for several blocks," replied Coleman.

Yates looked over his shoulder at the people in the club. "You know, I probably got this for a while." He looked back at his partner. "So, if you want to go spend some time with her, now's the time, Jim Bill."

Coleman grabbed Yates' hand and shook it with both of his own. "Thank you, Johnny, thank you! I really owe you one!"

Yates laughed. "You really got it bad, don't you? She's over there," he said, nodding his head in the girl's direction.

With a final smile at his partner, Coleman headed into the crowd, moving in the direction that Yates had indicated. After a moment of frenzied searching, he spotted her on the floor. Her back was to him.

Smiling, he crept up behind her and tapped her on the shoulder. She whirled so fast that it barely registered to him that she had turned! And her eyes...*was that a flash of* red *there?* If it was, it was gone now – the girl's eyes were back to their normal brown.

"Hi," she said. "You're back tonight."

Coleman nodded. "So are you," he said, smiling slightly.

The girl smiled, too. "I hoped you'd be here."

The music had stopped for a moment.

"Want to dance?" she asked.

"Sure!" replied Coleman excitedly. "By the way, what's your name? I'd love to know."

The music started as she spoke, so that Coleman could not understand what she said. It sounded very guttural, and full of consonants, and the girl was heading for the dance floor.

"Wait!" he called after her, as he followed. "What did you say? I didn't understand you!"

The girl ignored his call and turned to him with a smile. The music was too loud on the dance floor for conversation, so she just continued smiling at Coleman, and started to dance. He shrugged, and began dancing with her, gradually becoming mesmerized again. Finally, a slow song began. He took the girl into his arms, and they began to slow dance. He held her as closely as he could, pressing her body against his, hoping that she didn't notice his arousal. She began looking into his eyes, and he found himself moving forward slowly, until their lips touched lightly, tenderly...he brushed her lips with his tongue, and she opened her mouth slightly, inviting him. Coleman took full advantage of her invitation, and their kiss turned into something wild. He no longer cared that he was on the dance floor of a popular club, no longer cared about finding a killer, and no longer cared what anyone thought.

The kiss broke, and Coleman almost sagged to the floor. When he regained his balance, he whispered into her ear. "Come down to my place, baby...we'll make love." She looked into his eyes quickly, her eyes widened slightly. "I mean, if you...I thought you...I was only...," he stammered.

The girl only smiled, put her finger to his lips, and nodded.

Coleman took the girl's hand, and they walked quickly to the door. When they got to Yates, Coleman called out to him, "Had enough for one night, Johnny! I'm heading home!"

"But our shift isn't over! What'll the captain say?" Yates called back.

"Cover for me, will ya?"

Coleman could not remember how they got to his apartment, or how long it took. He was focused on one thing – making love to this beautiful, wild child. He led her to the bedroom. The girl walked to the far wall, and they stood a few feet apart.

"I hope this is okay," he said. "I only have a double bed...but the sheets are clean."

The girl giggled. "I suppose you want me to get undressed now?"

"Oh, yeah!" he said excitedly. "I mean, if you want to...I wanted..." He was stammering again.

"Isn't this what we came here for?" she asked. "Now calm down! You go first."

"Me?"

"Sure, silly!" She giggled again.

"O-okay." Coleman began fumbling with his clothes. The girl watched him, smiling at his seeming inexperience. Finally, he had everything off except his socks.

"Those, too." She looked at his socks.

Coleman quickly took them off. "Now it's your turn," he said rather breathlessly.

She smiled and kicked off her shoes. Then, with a playful look in her eyes, she turned her back. Her shorts came off first, and there was nothing on under them. Coleman couldn't take his eyes off of her bottom as she took off her blouse and bra, then crossed her arms over her chest, with her hands tucked under her hair on both sides. With her back still to him, she said, "I told you my name."

Coleman, still keeping a close watch on the girl's butt, said, "Yeah, but I didn't understand it."

Her hair flipped as she shook her head. "It doesn't matter. I told you my name. You see, with our people, when you learn our name, this *has* to happen."

"And I'm very glad."

"Come closer."

Coleman began moving toward her as she spoke. "You see now?" she asked. "Our people don't do this normally. But we've run out of food, and I had to come to the city to find some. But, when you learned my name, we had to come here."

Coleman was directly behind her. He reached for her hands to pull her into him. Her fingers had stiffened, and seemed to be about six inches long. His eyes widened in surprise as he parted her hair and saw the claws that had, just a couple of minutes ago, been her beautiful hands.

The girl whirled around. Her face had grown into a nightmarish horror, unbearable to look at, and somewhat lupine. Her eyes were glowing from some deep, inner orange fire. She shoved her claws into his rib cage, one hand on each side. Coleman's pain was a living thing as she moved close to him. She said, "I'm sorry. I will consume your liver...and your heart. Because, you see, once you have learned my name, your heart...," with tremendous strength, she pulled his rib cage open down the center of his chest, "...belongs to *ME!*"

She licked his blood from her lips and began to feed.

THE LION SLEEPS TONIGHT

Colonel Quentin James Abernathy (Ret.) poured tea into cups, and glanced at his guest from beneath bushy gray eyebrows.

Colonel Abernathy had retired from Her Majesty's service many years ago. His age was indeterminate, but, if the truth were known, the Colonel was well past ninety. He had retired a bachelor to a stately London townhouse, and lived comfortably with his pension, and his family fortune. He had several acquaintances from the club a few blocks away. One of them was sitting in his study, preparing to enjoy tea on a rainy afternoon.

Huffing into his large moustache, and speaking with a strong, gruff voice, Colonel Abernathy said, "Helmsley! Did I ever tell you the story of the stone lion?"

Helmsley shook his head. "No, Colonel, I can't say that you have."

"Help yourself to some biscuits. They're baked by my cook, and are quite satisfying. And please try the sandwiches...they're lemony cucumber and prawn. Very savory."

"Thank you, Colonel," said Helmsley.

Colonel Abernathy took a sip of tea. "Earl Grey, piping hot. Wonderful flavor, as always."

"It's quite good, Colonel."

The Colonel cleared his throat. "Hmm...yes...thank you." He adjusted himself into a more comfortable position. "Now, the story of the stone lion...," he began.

Many years ago, one of the Empire's colonies was in British Guyana in South America. I carried the rank of Major at that time, and was stationed on the Brazilian border, in charge of a garrison of lads. In the fifties, it was...and they were stout lads, every one. Even there, we were very close to the equator, and the humidity was quite overpowering. It took several days to acclimate ourselves to that horrid climate, and the insects were simply atrocious! We were surrounded by dense jungle, and the garrison was positioned beside a small river. The jungle grew so quickly that I had to assign lads for clearing duty every two days. A perimeter of a hundred yards all around was kept clear, and we had large machinery that helped us keep the road unobstructed.

We had several Wapishana natives that served as manservants within the garrison. They were quite good at taking care of the day-to-day workings, but they absolutely refused to go out at night! The only time that they would consider going outdoors after dark was the of the new moon.

I, of course, questioned them about this at length. For many weeks, they wouldn't give a reason. Finally, one man, the leader of the nearby village, disclosed the answer.

"The giant lion, sir," said the man...his name escapes me at the moment.

"Lion?" I replied in disbelief. "There are no lions in Guyana, or in South America, for that matter!"

"Er...more tea, Helmsley?" asked the Colonel.

"Yes, please. It's quite delicious, Colonel."

The Colonel may have smiled. Helmsley couldn't tell through the large moustache.

Colonel Abernathy poured more tea for his guest. As he placed the teapot back onto the tray, he said, "Now, where was I? Oh, yes!"

The man was quite insistent.

"Respectfully, sir, it is the giant lion. We do not go out in the moonlight. That is when the lion feeds."

I couldn't question the man further that day, as I had scheduled some maneuvers and exercises for the lads that afternoon. Nothing major, of course. Not in that godforsaken climate! Just enough to keep them sharp, you see. Guyana needed to be kept under control during that time. You understand.

A few days later, I received word from the Governor. He ordered us out on patrol for a fortnight. I immediately mobilized the men for an extended patrol, mostly on foot, so as to present a military presence to the locals. A squad of four lads, under the command of one Sergeant McBride, remained behind to secure the garrison.

At dawn the next morning, the lads and I were off on our patrol. We marched approximately twenty miles each day, displaying Her Majesty's finest all through the country. When we reached the Governor's residence, he received me with great enthusiasm, and served tea to several of my officers. Very pleasant man, congenial to a fault!

I gave the lads two nights of leave while we were in town. At dawn on the third day, we began our trip back to the garrison. I anticipated that it would take three days to arrive, and I was quite correct.

We arrived at the garrison at midday, and we were met by two things: the villagers, and tragedy.

"Please have more tea, Helmsley," said the Colonel.

"No, thank you, Colonel Abernathy. I must say that it's the best Earl Grey tea I've had in some time."

Colonel Abernathy waved his hand in dismissal. "No thanks necessary, Helmsley. My housekeeper found it at a quaint old tea shop not far from here. Shopkeeper makes it himself, he does." He huffed into his moustache again. "Normally, I would fire up my faithful Meerschaum...but, not allowed to have it anymore. Bloody doctors!"

As I was saying, we were met with villagers and tragedy. It seems that Sergeant McBride and his squad of lads had been massacred while we were out on our patrol!

The village leader...still can't remember his bloody name...met us a few yards from the entrance, and wouldn't let us enter the camp just yet. He told us what had happened, and said that, during the full moon, the giant lion had come into the garrison and killed all of the men.

"The screams could be heard plainly in the village, Major Abernathy," the native said. "We also heard several shots. We did not come to the garrison that night. We could not have saved them, so we chose to remain alive."

"Nonsense! What sort of gibberish are you telling me? *There are no lions in South America!*"

I was quite upset, and found myself shouting at the man. I couldn't believe what I thought was a simple native superstition, or, perhaps, a joke being performed for our benefit to cover up what, or who, really killed my men.

"Major, do you have a tracker in your unit? A man that can track things through the jungle?" asked the native, once I had stopped shouting.

"As a matter of fact, I do," I replied.

"Then, if you please, Major, bring him forward, and I will escort the two of you inside while the rest of your men remain outside. That way, the tracks will not be disturbed. You may decide for yourself what happened."

The man was quite earnest with his words, and I could see in his eyes that he thought he spoke the truth. I turned to the men.

"Leftenant Wilkins! Front and center, there's a good lad!"

The leftenant was an amazing tracker. He had once tracked a camel across the dunes of the Sahara. He quickly stepped forward at my command.

"Yes, sir!" he said briskly.

"You and I will accompany this man into the garrison. You are to scout about for tracks for indications of whatever killed our men." To the troops, I said, "The rest of you lads will remain outside the perimeter, and stand guard!"

The three of us entered the boundaries of the garrison. We walked slowly, as Leftenant Wilkins looked about for signs on the ground.

The villager said, "I arrived this morning, and entered the garrison alone, Major. I found the men just ahead. They're scattered, as if the lion played with them before it killed them. They put up quite a fight, from what the tracks indicate."

Just then, we came upon the slaughtered men. It was horrible, as they were torn into several pieces. Five men, whittled down to so much scattered meat...it was quite demoralizing.

The scene was as the villager had said. Empty brass cartidges were spread about, and it was obvious that the Sergeant had led a good fight, and the men had died with honor. I made a mental note to assign a burial detail, and I began thinking of the letters to the families of the downed lads that I would be forced to write.

Just then, the Leftenant called out.

"Major! You need to see this, sir!"

I briskly walked to the Leftenant's side. He pointed to the ground. There, outlined in the mud, was the print of a big cat, and it was as large as a mitt used in American baseball!

Several more tracks were strewn about, and the Leftenant read the story as if it were a book.

"The animal came from there," he pointed to the rear of the garrison, "and took the Sergeant and his men by surprise, sir. They were outside the barracks, perhaps trying to find a cooling breeze, or to smoke. If you'll look here," he again pointed to the ground, "the animal sprang at them. They fought well, sir, but it wasn't enough. When it was done, the animal returned the way it had come."

The Leftenant shook his head. "There's...one more thing, Major."

"What is it, Wilkins?"

"Sir, from the tracks, this thing is *enormous!* It looks to be over eight feet long, and, from the depth of the tracks, it weighs almost a thousand pounds!"

I had no reason to disbelieve the man. I had seen the paw print, and it only followed that the animal's size would match the print.

I turned to the village leader and offered my apologies for my original disbelief. He accepted quite gracefully.

I then asked the Leftenant if he could track the beast to its jungle hiding place.

"Yes, sir!"

"Very well. Here's what we will do: I want you to choose twenty of your best men. We'll leave at dawn. We simply cannot leave a beast of this size alive. Not since it has a taste for humans!"

Now came a different problem...I wanted the village leader to accompany us. I turned and asked the man if he would come with us, and, to my surprise, he said that he would.

I was astonished! The villagers were terrified of the beast, and this man was going to assist with finding and killing the animal!

I sent the Leftenant with orders to assign a burial squad, and that no man was to be outdoors after dark.

The Colonel's housekeeper, a portly matron named Mrs. Travers, came into the study to retrieve the tea tray.

"Colonel, will your guest be staying for dinner?" asked Mrs. Travers.

The Colonel glanced at the grandfather clock. "Great Scott! Helmsley, we've storied the afternoon away! You must let me see to your dinner!"

"I wouldn't want to be an imposition, Colonel," replied Helmsley.

"Nonsense! No imposition at all!" The Colonel twisted in his chair. "It's decided, then, Mrs. Travers. Helmsley will join us for dinner!"

Mrs. Travers nodded her understanding and left the study with the tea tray.

"Now, then...where the bloody blazes was I? Oh, yes..."

We left directly at dawn the next morning, with Leftenant Wilkins leading the way. I can't stress to you how dense that jungle could be, and we were walking through it, apparently following a game trail. Twenty-three men, and all were wary and alert for this giant killer! We were using machetes to hack away the underbrush that blocked our way as we tracked the beast to its lair.

Of course, a brief rain shower poured down as we hunted, but it wasn't hard enough to penetrate the canopy of leaves above us. At first, we heard many different animal sounds as we made our way through the jungle, but, as we proceeded, the animal sounds lessened until they were nonexistent. The only sound was the bloody insects! Apparently, nothing could chase them away!

Late that afternoon, just before teatime, we came upon the ruins of an ancient temple. Through the underbrush, we could see that the walls were still standing, but the roof had collapsed long ago.

Leftenant Wilkins showed me some tracks in the dirt, and said that the big cat had leapt to the top of the wall at this point.

I ordered the lads into the temple, explaining that we would make camp, and prepare tea. If enough sunlight remained, we would press on after that.

Within the walls of the temple, the Leftenant continued looking around as the other lads established a small camp. The animal's tracks led into another room of the temple. When he called me into the room, I saw that there were no other doors into it, and Wilkins pointed out that the tracks ended at the base of a huge stone statue.

I asked, "Did the beast leap onto the statue and out of the room?"

"No, sir," Wilkins replied. "No sign of that at all. Look at the statue, Major."

I had not even looked at the statue before the Leftenant pointed it out. It was a highly detailed, almost life-like statue of a great cat! I later found out that it was a representation of *Panthera leo atrox*...the American lion, which had been extinct for ten thousand years!

This lion was a good four feet tall at its shoulder. It was in a standing position, and its head was even with my chin! It was a huge beast! One man would never be a match for this beast alone!

I heard a gasp behind us. Wilkins and I whirled to see the village leader staring fearfully at the statue.

With a stammer, the native said, "Th-th-that's the lion, Major. The one that prowls in the moonlight!"

"But it's only a statue!" I exclaimed.

"The legend passed down to us is that when the tiniest bit of moonlight strikes the creature, it becomes a real lion, and remains that way until dawn!" he explained.

Having doubted the man once before and been proven wrong, I hesitated to disagree with what the leader said...although, the idea of a stone figure coming to life was difficult to believe.

I immediately ordered every man jack of our lads into position with all of their weapons at the ready to await the rising of the moon.

We didn't have a long wait.

As ridiculous as it sounded, when the first sparkle of moonlight struck the stone beast, it became alive.

I won't go into details, as they're quite disturbing...and I have difficulties speaking of what happened next, but the carnage was astounding.

The lion immediately pounced into the midst of the lads. It was fired upon at least fifty times, but it was obviously impervious to bullets. Its hatred was very visible in its eyes. One by one, the lion tore the men apart. By the time I called a retreat, only myself, Wilkins, the native, and two men were able to flee.

We gained the outside of the temple with the lion in hot pursuit. It took first one, then the other enlisted man. We three made it to a group of very tall, very thin trees, and we immediately began climbing!

The lion was stopped! It could not climb the thin trees because of its weight, nor could it reach us, as we were in the highest branches above the beast.

There we remained until dawn's first light. The lion returned to its post inside the temple, and became stone once more.

"What happened to the lion, Colonel?" asked Helmsley.

The Colonel chuckled into his mustache. "Come with me, Helmsley, I want to show you something." The Colonel rose stiffly from his chair, and led the way to a hallway that ended at a locked door.

"Once we had climbed down, we immediately returned to the garrison," continued the Colonel. "On the next new moon, I took fifty men through the jungle, and returned to the temple. We loaded it with explosives, blew the place to pieces, and buried the remaining stones."

"So, the threat was ended, then. Jolly good reasoning, Colonel!"

The Colonel unlocked the door they were facing, opened it, then fumbled at the inside wall until he found the light switch, and clicked it on.

Inside was a totally windowless room. Ceiling-to-floor shelves made of rich mahogany lined the walls of the room. Many curiosities were spread about the room, including a suit of armor, and, of all things, a coffin!

Directly placed in the center of the room was a huge, highly detailed statue of *Panthera leo atrox* – the American Lion.

"I had the statue crated up at my own expense, informing the men that no light whatsoever must penetrate the interior of the packing crate. I then had the statue shipped here, where it has remained safely for all these many years. There are no windows in this room, so that no moonlight can possibly reach the beast!" explained Colonel Abernathy. "I don't know what magic placed the spirit of a long-extinct beast inside this stone prison, but I couldn't take the risk that blowing the statue apart might release the creature permanently."

Helmsley said with awe, "Amazing, Colonel!" He examined the details of the statue. "It's incredibly life-like!" He took a moment to glance around the room. "Colonel, what of these other curiosities? Are there stories behind these, as well?"

The Colonel chuckled as he led the way from the room, and locked the door behind them. "Those, my good friend, are stories for another time! Come, let us have dinner, and, perhaps, a brandy afterward. I," he paused for a moment, "*may* be persuaded to share another story with you then."

The two men walked down the hall to the dining room, and the Colonel did indeed tell another tale.

A tale both *of* another time, and *for* another time.

DON'T COME AROUND HERE NO MORE

A TALE OF SARDIS COUNTY

"I don't give a rat's ass what you're lookin' for!" shouted the skinny, grizzled old man. "Don't come around here no more!"

The old man was dressed in patched, faded jeans, a stained, white button-up shirt, and an old tattered black vest. His hair was gray, long, and unkempt. He hadn't shaved in several days, and age spots gave him a dirty appearance. Thick, round spectacles on his face gave his eyes an owlish look. He stood on the sagging front porch of his deteriorating home, having just climbed from his faded rocking chair. What little paint remained on the wooden siding was peeling, pieces of the porch roof were dangling, and the house was missing a shingle here and there. Trees surrounded the house on both sides and the back of the four acre lot, giving the house the feeling of a tattered cabin in the backwoods, instead of a domicile on a southern city street. The front of the house had a rickety wooden picket fence along the sidewalk, with an unlatched gate at the center. The yard was as scraggly and unkempt as its owner.

The objects of the old man's anger stood at the gate, not believing what the old man was saying to them.

The three high school seniors, Terry Patterson, Clay Bowman, and Joni Ragsdale, were a team, and had been given a social studies assignment as their final exam grade. Each team of three seniors would be given an address of someone in the small town's city limits that appeared to need repair and upkeep, with the idea that those who are needy should be helped by those that are able. The school would provide materials, the students would provide labor, and Mr. Hendrix's observation would provide the addresses for each team of three. There were eight teams, and each team had three months to complete the assignment, at absolutely no cost to the homeowner.

No one anticipated that a homeowner would turn down free home improvement, but that's what this grizzled old man was apparently doing.

Joni, the sweet-talker of the group, tried to explain. "But, sir, it won't cost you a dime! All we want to do is fix up your house! It's for our senior social studies project!"

The old man waved a fist at them. "I told you, I don't give a rat's ass what you want! Don't come around here no more!"

The young people looked around at each other and shrugged. They had no choice – they had to leave. Clay had driven over, so they got back into his car and drove away. The old man watched them as they left.

"Well, that was weird," said Clay.

"I never expected anybody to turn down free work," said Joni.

Terry still was shaking his head. "I bet Mr. Hendrix never expected this."

"Hey, do you think that guy didn't believe us?" asked Joni

Clay laughed. "With a trunk so loaded down with paint, rollers, boards, and other stuff that it won't even close? You're kidding, right?"

"Maybe he thought we stole it," Joni replied.

"Whatever he thought, let's go back to school to tell Mr. Hendrix. Maybe he can talk to the guy or something," declared Terry. "We have to do something. Our grades, and our graduation, depend on fixing up somebody's house."

Mr. Hendrix did indeed want to talk to the man, just to make certain that he understood that the repairs done by the students wouldn't cost him a dime. Materials were either donated by businesses in the city of Perry, or purchased with cash donations, and students performed the labor. He asked the students to follow him back to the old man's house, but to wait in the car until he had spoken with the man.

Andy Hendrix was one of Perry High School's favorite teachers. The kids respected him, because he didn't mind going to bat for them if they were in the right, or helping them if they showed him that they really wanted to learn. He had taught different levels of American history, and assorted social studies courses for over twelve years now, and he was proud of the job he'd done, and was doing, for his students.

This particular social studies project had originally come about as an idea Hendrix had ten years earlier as he was driving home. He had noticed several houses along his route home that needed small amounts of upkeep. From time to time, he noticed the homeowners outside. Most were elderly, obviously living on a fixed income, or people that had been laid off from Perry's only remaining industry: a meat processing plant that had been taken over by robotics and automation. The few people the plant used were of Hispanic heritage, and would work for minimum wage.

Many farms were still operating in Sardis County, but very few were still family-owned. Most had been taken over by large conglomerates, much like the processing plant.

As a result of the lack of jobs and money in Perry, Hendrix had gone to a meeting of the Perry Board of Alderman.

By the time he was called to say what was on his mind, he had a well-thought-out plan to present to the Board. He passed out a folder with copies of his proposal.

"Ladies and gentlemen, what you have in front of you is a proposal that will help our poor and needy citizens, and our high school seniors, and will raise property values in Perry," said Hendrix.

"The idea is, basically, to have our high school seniors split into teams of three. Using materials donated by Perry businesses, or purchased by donations from parents and businesses, these teams of high school seniors will, as part of their final grade, perform minor upkeep on the homes of retired folks on fixed incomes and on the homes of those that have been laid off from their jobs.

"By doing this within a frame of three months or so, these seniors will learn the true meaning of 'social studies' by learning that helping others also helps themselves. Fixed income retirees will have a little extra money to spend in town, and so will those living on unemployment. It also will raise property values in the city by upkeep on the residences. For just a little paint, lumber, nails, and tools, the city of Perry, and the entire county, will reap the benefits."

Members of the board had only a few questions, easily answered by Hendrix. They voted that very night to give the proposal their unanimous stamp of approval, pending passage by the Sardis County School Board, and a hearing by the Chamber of Commerce.

Both of those organizations heartily approved the proposition. The Sardis County School Board insisted that he implement the program as soon as possible. Hendrix wasted no time in preparing it for the next full school year.

Most of the county read about the program in a write-up in the Sardis County Sentinel (Sardis County – Where YOU Make The Magic!), the county's weekly newspaper. Some heard about it on the county's small radio station.

Very few didn't know about the program.

Residents often petitioned Hendrix, asking that their house be part of the current year's project. So many petitioned Hendrix, and became angry as a result of his refusal to include them, that county officials announced that they had demanded that Hendrix not tell anyone which houses had been chosen for the school year. That included the recipients, which explained why the old man had chased the kids away...he didn't know that the project had chosen his address.

After the young people reported back to him, Hendrix did some research on the address he'd assigned to the students. The owner of the property was registered as Ricky Jackson. Mr. Jackson had owned the home for forty years, his taxes were up to date, and there were no liens on the property. Mr. Jackson's wife had passed away a few years ago, and he lived alone.

Armed with this information, Hendrix was ready to talk to Mr. Ricky Jackson.

The two cars pulled to a stop at the curb a bit farther down from Mr. Jackson's home. Hendrix climbed out, and walked to the other car.

"Okay, guys, just stay here until I come back," Hendrix told the three young people.

"Sir, are you sure you don't want us to come with you?" asked Joni.

Hendrix smiled. "Thanks, but I think I'd better talk to him alone." He banged his hand twice, lightly, on the door frame. "Be back shortly."

As they watched their teacher walk to the house, Joni said, "I hope he can't convince that old guy. I don't like his house...and I don't like him, either."

Clay turned to look at her from the driver's seat. "Why, Joni?"

Joni wrinkled her mouth and shook her head. "I don't know...there's just something...dark, maybe, about that house."

Terry, the jock of the bunch, said, "Maybe that old man is a killer, and he's buried bodies in the yard somewhere!"

Joni shuddered. "Stop it, Terry! I'm freaked enough!"

Andy Hendrix never considered himself a superstitious man, but something made the hairs on the back of his neck stand up as he climbed the steps to Jackson's porch. He felt watched...like he was in danger, somehow. Nothing seemed out of the ordinary, except a lot of peeling paint and sagging porch boards.

Hendrix knocked on the front door. He stood with his hands at his sides, waiting, with his school ID in his hand. He heard footsteps inside, a chain being removed, and a deadbolt being thrown. The door slowly opened.

The haggard old man, Ricky Jackson, stood in the doorway, staring at the uninvited guest on his front porch. Hendrix noted that the man was as unkempt as the kids had described.

As he introduced himself, Hendrix held out his ID for the man to see. "Sir, my name is Andy Hendrix. I teach history and social studies at Perry High School."

Jackson leaned over and studied the ID through his thick spectacles. When he finished, he stood upright, and asked, "What's it to me?"

"Mr. Jackson, I'm sure you know about our annual project involving some of our high school seniors. They are assigned an address in Perry, and are given three months to perform minor upkeep on the residence at that address, using materials given to them by businesses and purchased by money collected for the project. The entire project is done at no cost to the homeowner." He looked Jackson in the eye. "Your house was one of the addresses chosen for this year."

Jackson's eyes widened. "You're talkin' about them kids that I ran off yesterday, aren't ya?"

Hendrix nodded. "I am. They're the team that's been assigned to your address."

Jackson cackled, and in between breaths, he said, "Oh, you shoulda seen their faces, Hendrix! They was so down that jumper cables wouldn't have got them back up!" He continued laughing.

Hendrix smiled. "So I take it that you don't mind them doing their project with you?"

Jackson's face sobered. "As long as...well, I don't need to tell it twice." He pointed toward Clay's car. "I see 'em peekin' through, there...tell 'em to come up here and I'll give 'em what they need to know."

Hendrix, puzzled, called the seniors to the porch. Terry, ever the athlete, walked briskly to the porch. Joni seemed to hang back a little, and Clay, who had more than a crush on the girl, walked with her.

Once the young people were at the porch, Hendrix said, "Now, Mr. Jackson has agreed to let you do some work on his home, but he wants to speak to you first. Mr. Jackson?" Four pairs of eyes turned to Jackson.

Jackson looked at each of them in turn. "Ground rules is this: you only work outside the house. You don't come in, no matter what. If you gotta use the bathroom, there's a store up the street on the corner...or, use a tree in the back. Nobody'll see.

"This house has a basement, and I got a...dawg...down there, so don't open no basement windows, and don't go in. That dawg's a character, and will try to get you to come inside and...play...with him. Don't do it. Whatever you see or hear, *don't go in that basement!* Or the house! If that's okay with you, and you fer sure can honor my wishes, then you can fix up the outside of this old shack."

Hendrix turned to his students, and spread his hands. "There you have it. I don't see a need to enter the house at all, do you?"

Joni shook her head, and the young men both said, "No, sir!"

Hendrix turned back to Jackson. "It seems that all of our problems have been agreed upon, Mr. Jackson. The kids will be here tomorrow right after lunch – it's part of the senior schedule for those that take my class. That'll be about one o'clock."

Jackson nodded sharply, unkempt hair nodding with his head. "Just mind my wishes...it's all I ask."

At lunch the next day, the three sat together in the school cafeteria.

Joni Ragsdale had always been a bookworm. She never asked questions in class, or volunteered anything, but her grades were all A's...which put her on the college path, and made her a member of the Perry High School Beta Club. Dark hair, well-brushed and stylish, hung to the middle of her back. She often wore her hair in a ponytail, as she had today, when she knew that she'd be doing something that loose hair might interfere with. She was an attractive girl, with small, almost elfin features, and wore minimal makeup.

Clay Bowman described himself as average. He had dark blond hair, and strong facial features. Clay didn't play sports, but his grades also made him a member of the Beta Club.

Clay and Joni were a couple, and had been for as long as anyone could remember. It was one of those cases – they knew they were right for each other from the time they met. They only had eyes for each other, and no one else had ever been able to turn their heads.

Terry Patterson was all about sports. He had played football all through high school, and played baseball his sophomore and junior years. He was an affable young man, with longish blonde hair, good looks, and a muscular build that some grown men envied. His grades weren't so hot, but he had been close friends with Clay and Joni since kindergarten, so he had a lot of help with his school work. He had full athletic scholarship offers from several distinguished colleges, but had not chosen one. He planned to wait until Joni and Clay had chosen their schools, and go from there.

All three were greeted occasionally by other students passing by as the three friends ate their lunches. The discussion topic, of course, turned to the house...and to Jackson.

"I have a bad feeling about that house," said Joni. "And Mr. Jackson seems so...sinister."

The guys broke out laughing.

"*Sinister?*" asked Terry, still laughing. "Where did you dig *that* word up?"

Joni looked smug. "I never thought I'd have a chance to use it. But it sure fits that guy!"

"Lots of people don't bathe every day, honey," said Clay. "That doesn't mean they're bad people."

"Yeah," said Terry. "Just stinky."

"What do you think about the dog?" asked Joni. "Think it's real?"

Terry shook his head. "Nah, I think he's growing pot in his basement."

All three laughed.

"Oh, well, whatever it is, we only have three months with it at the most," said Clay.

The seniors arrived at Jackson's house at one o'clock. They began unloading gallons of paint, brushes, and rollers from Clay's car trunk, and then untied the ladder from the roof.

Jackson was sitting in his battered rocking chair on the front porch, watching their every move. As the young people began bringing their supplies into the yard, Joni noticed that not only did Jackson still seem 'sinister', as she put it, but he also seemed tired...and *frightened?* Was that fear she saw in his face?

What's he afraid of? she thought to herself. *I don't know if I like that.*

Terry spoke to the old man. "Hello, sir, here we are."

"We thought we'd start on the front, if that's okay with you, Mr. Jackson," continued Clay. "We guessed that if the front looks good, it will give us more time to work on the rest of the house."

Jackson waved impatiently at them. "Sure, go ahead, whatever you want to do. I'll be inside." He rose from his rocker and went inside. He closed the door firmly behind him.

The group exchanged looks.

"Ohhhh-kay," said Terry. He looked at Clay. "Front wall first?"

Clay nodded. "Yeah. Joni can paint the windows and the trim."

Joni looked at the two guys. "Well, thanks for telling me what I *can* do!" She picked up the power saw. "I'm not painting squat right now...I'll be repairing the broken boards!"

The next couple of hours, the seniors worked hard on the front of the house. They sawed, painted, hammered, and straightened, until four o'clock rolled around. That was their designated time to leave.

The young people didn't know where to store the supplies, so Terry knocked on the front door.

Jackson opened it almost immediately, as if he had been watching them through the front door window.

"What is it, young'un?" asked Jackson.

"Sir, is there someplace out of the way that we can store our supplies? We can't bring them back and forth to school with us, and we can't leave them in the yard," said Terry.

Jackson studied the seniors for a moment, then pointed to the far end of the porch. "Stack 'em on that end, if you want. Lemme see what you've done so far." He came out onto the porch and shut the door behind him. He looked around the porch for several minutes, and, when he turned, he couldn't speak very well.

"Ahem...[cough]...it's looking pretty good, kids. Thank you," stammered Jackson.

Terry, trying to distract the old man's emotion, replied, "Well, the painting is only the first coat, sir. To do it right will take at least one more coat, if not two. It hadn't been painted in such a long time, that the wood is soaking the paint in almost as fast as we get it covered. Joni repaired the loose boards, and replaced a couple that weren't safe. Clay and I painted them. We still have the part above the porch to paint, but we'll tackle that tomorrow, then let the front dry. After that, we'll start on the sides."

Jackson peered over his glasses at Joni. "You mean, *she* did the carpentering?"

Joni actually smiled at Jackson as she nodded. "I did, sir. My dad owns one of the lumber supply places here in Perry. He's taught me a lot."

"What's your name, girl?" asked Jackson.

"Joni Ragsdale, sir."

Jackson's eyes widened. "Ragsdale? Ragsdale Lumber and Supply? That's your people?"

Joni nodded.

"I used to run around with your Grandpa. Me and him were really close for a while." The old man lowered his eyes. "Damn heart attack took him way too soon."

"Thank you, sir."

"Well, I'd help you kids, but when you're my age...," Jackson started.

He was interrupted by an extremely loud howl that ended with a deep, throaty growl. It didn't sound exactly like a dog...but, at the same time, it did.

The kids all exchanged looks. The howl, however, deeply disturbed Jackson. Joni thought, *It's almost like it...*scares *him!*

Jackson spoke as the throaty growl ended. "Okay, kids, okay...get yer stuff and put it there," he pointed toward the end of the porch, "and I'll s-s-see you t-tomorrow. I gotta go see the damned thing and calm it down!"

Joni took a step forward. "Sir, with all due respect, Clay has a way with animals, if you'd like him to..."

"NO!" Jackson shouted. "I'll see to it, you kids get on out of here for today! I'll see you tomorrow at one." With that, Jackson slammed the front door behind him as he went inside.

The seniors started to stack their supplies. When they were almost finished, they heard the howl again. It wasn't a plaintive howl. It sounded eager, almost excited, and sent chills down the kids' backs.

Clay said quietly, "That's no dog."

"What do you mean, it's no dog?" asked Terry.

"Just what I said," replied Clay. "It's nothing that I've ever heard before. Not dog, not wolf, not coyote. I don't know what it is, but I know what it isn't."

They finished hurriedly, and almost ran to the car.

The next day, at lunch again, Joni brought up the subject that they all had been avoiding.

"So, boys, should we tell Mr. Hendrix about the howl?"

Clay and Terry exchanged glances.

"I don't think we should," replied Terry.

"Not yet, anyway," added Clay.

"You guys sure?" asked Joni.

Both boys nodded.

"I'd like to hear it again...see if maybe it's something I can figure out," said Clay.

Joni shrugged. "Okay, but I'm still creeped out about the whole thing."

But, when they got to Jackson's house, Jackson was sitting on his front porch, quietly reading a book, and they heard no howl that day...or the next. Then came the weekend.

Andy Hendrix did not require his social studies students to work on their projects on weekends, but he pointed out, correctly, that many repairs were simply too time-consuming to be done in a few afternoons. Once started, some projects had to be continued until they were completed. Not every team had projects that were that lengthy, but many did.

The three young people had chosen to work that Saturday, from nine in the morning until four that afternoon. They had planned to paint one side of Jackson's house, with two full coats of paint. Jackson's house stretched back along his property for at least fifty feet, and they wouldn't have come close to finishing the paint job in one after-school afternoon.

On Friday, Jackson had given his approval for the Saturday work. Since all three seniors were driving individually, Jackson had also given them permission to park their cars in his driveway, instead of along the curb.

Terry led the way, while Clay and Joni followed in Clay's car. They pulled into Jackson's driveway, and climbed out, ready to work.

Jackson was sitting on his porch, reading a book again. As the seniors passed by him with mumbled "Good morning" greetings, Jackson waved at them. Just as they began moving their supplies to the left side of the house, the howl came: loud, long, enthusiastic, and unlike anything any of them had ever heard before. Hairs rose on all three seniors' necks, and Jackson looked almost panicked. He quickly rose from his rocking chair, and ran inside the house, slamming the door behind him.

"Clay, I can't do this! What *is* that howling?" said Joni, as she held both of Clay's hands in hers.

Clay put his arms around Joni and held her tightly for a moment, then held her by the shoulders.

"Whatever it is, Joni, we still have to complete our project. Now, come on – I'm here, Terry's here, and we won't let anything happen to you."

"Clay's right," added Terry. "Nothing will get past us."

After a couple of deep breaths, Joni nodded. "Okay. Let's go."

Between the three of them, they were able to carry everything that they'd need to get started, including the ladder. Clay and Joni had the ladder, and Terry led the way with brushes, rollers, and paint. As they rounded the corner of the house, Terry stopped abruptly, and Joni almost ran into him with the ladder.

"What's wrong with you, Terry? Why'd you stop?" Joni asked.

Terry didn't say anything. He only raised his arm and pointed.

Clay and Joni followed his finger. Ahead of them, about twenty feet from where they stood, a small rectangular window, a little longer than a shoebox and half again as wide, was open at ground level. It was obviously a vent window for the basement. Jackson's voice could be heard through the open window, but they couldn't understand words.

Whispering, Terry said, "Let's go peek."

"No!" whispered Joni urgently. "Mr. Jackson told us not to look in the basement!"

"No, he didn't," replied Clay. "He said don't go into the house, don't go down to the basement, and don't open any basement windows. He did *not* say we couldn't look inside if there was *already* an open window." Clay looked at Joni. "A technicality, yes, but I'm still going to look!"

"Me, too!" added Terry.

Joni shook her head at the stupidity of boys. "Okay, but just a quick peek!"

They crept closer. Jackson's voice became clearer the closer they got.

"...don't wanna hear no more of...I've heard enough! You're scaring those kids and you're going to annoy the neighbors to the point that the police'll show up! I just need a few more days, and I'll send you right back to Hell, you damned hound! I wish I could kill you right now, but I know I can't!"

Clay tensed up at these words.

The seniors were right outside the window now. Along with Jackson's words, they could hear a low grunting, and an occasional snarling sound...almost a growl.

Jackson's tirade against the basement's resident had continued nonstop.

Terry knelt on one side of the rectangular window, and Clay knelt on the other side. They eased their heads slowly until they could see inside. Both of the young men's mouths slowly dropped open, and their eyes grew as wide as saucers. Joni sighed with frustration, then knelt beside Clay, and eased her head around his until she could see, too.

Jackson was standing just inches outside of a large pentagram that had at least a ten foot diameter. Pacing within the confines of the pentagram was a huge creature that defied description. Larger than a St. Bernard, the creature had a long, almost serpentine neck. Its eyes faced forward, and glowed with a deep, greenish light. Its snout was almost lupine, with wolf ears and a mouthful of needle-like teeth. With so many teeth, the creature's mouth wouldn't close all the way, and it drooled constantly, but the drool never hit the floor – it disappeared before it fell that far. It had a long, thin lion's tail, and growing from its back were two large bat wings that it could fold against its body. Its skin appeared to the shocked onlookers to be rough and pebbly, much like a rhinoceros's skin. When the creature uttered its snarl, its tongue came out, and appeared to be long and snakelike.

Joni's mouth opened wide, and her eyes grew larger, too. But, she made the mistake of letting out a surprised gasp. The creature heard this, and its head whipped around toward the noise. This got Jackson's attention, and he turned to the window. When he saw the young people peering in through the window, his face expressed outrage. He pointed to them, about to start shouting. He didn't notice that his arm extended over the line of pentagram.

The creature noticed. Almost faster than the eye could follow, it whipped its head around, opened its mouth, and bit down on Jackson's arm. Blood erupted from the old man's arm and sprayed into the creature's mouth. Jackson began screaming and trying to get his arm away from the creature. He was not succeeding.

The creature was grunting, seemingly with pleasure.

Joni hit Clay's arm. "We have to do something!"

The three young people ran to the front door, flung it open, and found the basement door. They threw it open and dashed down the stairs.

Jackson's screams had become hoarse, but he was still gallantly fighting to retrieve his arm.

Terry hurriedly looked around the basement. Jackson's washer and dryer were tucked under the basement stairs, and he found a bath towel on top of the dryer. He grabbed it, and held one end in each hand. He twirled it to give it a smaller, more compact size. Moving beside Jackson, Terry snapped the towel directly into the creature's right eye. The creature let go of Jackson's arm to snap at the towel, and Terry dropped the towel. He and Clay helped the old man away from the creature. They stretched him out onto the floor, with his back against a large chest freezer.

Joni examined the wound on Jackson's arm. It was deep, with several puncture marks in a semicircle, both on top and below. It was bleeding, but not badly.

Joni took Jackson's face and turned it so that she could look directly into his eyes. "Mr. Jackson! Where can I find first aid?"

"H-huh?" the old man stammered.

"First aid, sir. Where is it?"

Jackson gestured with his uninjured arm. "Top of the basement stairs...bathroom cabinet."

Joni looked at Clay, who nodded and ran up the stairs.

"You kids...now you...oh, it's all my fault," said Jackson weakly.

"Try not to talk, Mr. Jackson," said Terry. "Not yet."

"Terry, would you please see if Mr. Jackson has more towels?"

"Sure, Joni."

Clay came down the stairs with his arms loaded down with antiseptics, antibiotic cream, gauze, cotton, and white tape. Terry came back with extra towels, and a bottle of water. Joni went to work on Jackson's arm.

Terry opened the water and held it to the old man's lips. "Drink some of this, Mr. Jackson."

Jackson drank a couple of sips of water. "Thank you, Terry."

Terry smiled. "You're welcome, sir."

The creature chose that moment to throw its head back and utter another one of those long, loud howls. All four of the humans in the basement jumped, because they weren't expecting the sudden noise. After the howl died down, Jackson looked at the three young people.

"I suppose you want to know what that is, since the secret ain't a secret anymore," he said.

Joni, focused on applying gauze bandages, murmured, "It's a Hellhound, isn't it, sir? I've seen pictures in some of Father Michael's books."

Jackson nodded.

"My wife passed away some years ago, kids. I got to missing her really bad a couple of months ago. Someday, you three will maybe be lucky enough to know a true soul-mate love like I had with Gina. When we were young...oh, it seems like just yesterday! Oh, you gotta treasure every moment...time is like a thief in the night, stealing away everything that matters to you! You kids don't know nothin' about that, of course."

Joni snuck a glance at Clay. Clay was looking at her and smiling. Joni returned the smile.

"Anyway, because I was missing Gina so bad, I went to this scary witch-woman that lives in the woods, and asked for a summoning spell. She gave me one, all right...only it didn't summon Gina like I wanted. I wasn't *specific* with the witch lady, you see. What she gave me was a summoning spell, all right...and a spell that opens a door into Hell. So, when I finished the spell, what shows up? Not Gina, like I wanted...nope, I get *this* damned thing!" He gestured toward the creature. "He's harmless enough, I guess. As long as the line around the pentagram stays intact, he can't come out. Oh, he wants to – he wants to real bad! But, as long as the line lasts, he can't come out. But, if something goes *in*, like some damn fool's arm that I could tell you about, it's Katie-bar-the-door! He can do what he does best! Ow! Hell! That's a little tight, Joni!"

"Sorry, Mr. Jackson," Joni replied. "I just want to make sure that the bandage is secure."

"Okay," replied Jackson. "That's okay, then."

"So," said Terry, "Why don't you send it back? Close the doorway?"

"Hell, boy, don't you think I would if I could?" Jackson snickered to himself. "Old witch-woman got the best of me, all right...told me how to open it, but didn't bother to tell me how to close it, or even how to send that damned Hellhound back!"

"If I understand you," said Clay, "As long as that pentagram stays there, that thing can't leave the circle?"

"Right."

"Then leave it alone! Don't come down here, ignore the thing when you *do* have to come down here! Eventually, it will get bored and go away!"

Jackson began shaking his head even before Clay finished. "Won't work, son...tried it. It howls when I ignore it."

"Do you feed it?" asked Terry.

Jackson laughed derisively. "Only when I'm dumb enough to stick my arm in front of it."

Joni asked, "Have you been back to see the woman that gave you the spell?"

"Of course, honey. But she's a witch-woman – the only one that Sardis County has ever had. If she don't want to be found, she ain't found! I've been back out there three times, and even her house is gone, like it's never been there!"

The creature had started pacing around its circle again, grunting and snarling. Its eyes were fastened on the four people, and its tongue was flicking in and out.

Joni turned to Jackson. "Do you want to try seeing her with us? We'll go with you, if you'd like."

Jackson looked up at her. "Would you? Really?"

Terry said, "Sure! It might help you, so why not?"

"Then, let's go. If you kids will help me up off this floor first."

Terry and Clay each took one arm and helped Jackson to his feet. Joni was picking up the first aid items and towels that were stained with Jackson's blood.

"Joni, just put them towels over by the washer," said Jackson. "I'll take care of them later." He looked at the three young people. "Do you see now why I told you don't come around here no more? I was afraid you'd get hurt, or run off to the po-lice. How do you tell folks you got a Hellhound in your basement?"

Joni started following the guys up the basement stairs. The creature gave out one last howl, and Joni turned back to look at it. She noticed that the towel Terry used to hit the creature in the eye was still on the basement floor.

"Terry," she said. "Would you mind picking up that last towel and putting it by the washer?"

"Sure thing!" Terry trotted down the stairs and over to the towel.

When Terry flicked the towel into the creature's eye, the creature released Jackson's arm, and Terry had dropped the towel to help Clay catch Jackson and pull him away. The towel now resided half in and half out of the pentagram. Rather than risk being bitten, Terry bent down and grabbed one corner of the towel that was on the outside, and gave it a brisk jerk backwards. He now had the towel, and was walking toward the washer.

The creature froze, looking down at the pentagram. Joni, still watching the creature, looked at what had caught its attention. Her eyes widened, and her face paled.

She tried to get her voice to work, but terror wouldn't let it. "*Run,*" she whispered.

Terry had returned to the bottom of the stairs and saw Joni's face. "What's wrong, Joni?"

Joni pointed as she finally got her voice to work. "*RUN!*" she screamed.

Terry looked back. The towel had erased a portion of the pentagram when Terry had pulled it back.

The creature howled again with eagerness, and leapt at Terry. Before Terry could move, the creature had buried its teeth into Terry's throat.

"He's done for! Joni, come on! Now!" urged Jackson.

Joni finally noticed that Terry wasn't moving, and his eyes were glazed over. He was dead. The creature turned its eyes upward and met Joni's. The green glow was unsettling, and a little bit...hypnotizing...maybe it...

"JONI!" yelled Clay. "We have to GO!"

Clay's urgency snapped Joni out of the creature's spell. She dropped the first aid supplies and ran up the stairs.

The creature leapt for her, but its wings got caught in the supports between the stairs and the floor above. By the time it figured out that it couldn't fly yet, and would have to climb the stairs, Joni had reached the top. Jackson slammed the door behind her.

The three people ran to Jackson's front door. Just as they opened it, something slammed against the basement door. They slammed the front door behind them.

Clay shouted, "Get to the car!"

The three got into Clay's car. Jackson's door in the back was slamming as Clay got the engine started. He shifted into reverse, and Jackson's front door crashed outwards, shattered pieces of wood and glass spreading out over the yard as shrapnel. The creature followed, bellowing its frustration at not catching the three. Clay stepped on the gas, and the car leapt backward into the street. The creature started flapping its huge batwings, and lifted off. Clay shifted into drive, and fed more gas, speeding toward Main Street.

"Joni, get your phone! Call the Perry Police Department and tell them that I'm coming past them in just a few minutes. Get them to shoot at the creature if they can!" said Clay.

"No! No po-lice!" said Jackson.

"Our friend is dead! We can't cover that up, Mr. Jackson!" replied Clay.

Joni was speaking into the cell phone. "Then just come outside and look!" she yelled.

KLA-BOOMP!

Something had hit the top of their car. The weight pushed the car down on its springs, and then it bounced back. It was obvious that the creature had tapped the car, and was keeping up easily, even though Clay was doing sixty.

"Oh, crap!" said Clay.

"What is it?" asked Joni.

"We only have a quarter of a tank. We better find that witch fast!"

KLA-BOOMP!

The car bounced again.

"Police station coming up on the right," said Clay.

Joni could see the station from her side. "A couple of cops are outside the station!"

Jackson suggested, "Honk your horn! They'll see it then!"

Clay laid on his horn. There were more cops outside than a couple...at least five had stopped what they were doing to look at the speeding car coming their way.

KLA-BOOMP! The rear window shattered, and the car's roof settled considerably.

The creature had settled on top of the car.

The cops all had amazed, unbelieving looks on their faces.

The creature's claws pierced the roof. Joni screamed.

As they passed the police station, the weight on top of the car disappeared, as did the claws in the roof. Clay could see in the passenger rear view mirror that the creature had pounced on one of the cops, and was ripping the cop to shreds. The others were firing their weapons into the creature, with no result.

Clay felt sorry for the cop, but it was their chance. He took an immediate right turn, and began speeding up to put some distance between them and the Hellhound.

"Where does the witch live, Mr. Jackson?" asked Clay.

Jackson told him.

In Jackson's basement, a strange mist was seemingly billowing from the floor within the pentagram. It hugged the floor of the basement, almost completely covering Terry Patterson's lifeless body.

An arm, almost as big around as Terry's body, and with a huge, clawed hand, rose from the mist around the pentagram...then slammed down onto the basement floor, as if it was seeking a hold to pull itself out.

"I'm telling you, it's in this clearing," said Jackson. "I may be old, but my memory still works!"

Jackson, Clay, and Joni had abandoned the car when they got to the woods. It was just as well, because they couldn't drive any further. The roof was badly dented, the rear window was gone, and the car was running on fumes. By Jackson's account, the woman's house was in the woods, and a person had to hike to a clearing about half a mile inside the woods to find it.

"I believe you, sir," said Joni. "But, we have to find a way to contact her."

"Yeah, before that Hellhound gets through with those cops and decides to track us down again!" said Clay.

Spring was just starting, and the leaves on the trees surrounding the clearing dappled the sunshine onto the green plants below. The clearing had new green grass, and the sun shone brightly down.

"There's something not quite right about this clearing," said Clay. "Give me a minute, and I'll figure out what it is."

"Hurry, Clay," said Joni quietly.

Clay studied the clearing, then said, "Mr. Jackson, did you ever cross the clearing?"

"Whaddaya mean, 'cross it'?"

"Did you ever try to walk from here to the other side?"

"No, I just stopped here, then turned around and went back once I saw that the house was gone."

Clay nodded. "I don't think it's gone. I think it's right here, and always has been." He bent to the ground, then stood again. "Let me show you."

Being best friends with Terry had taught Clay a few things, like how to throw a baseball. Clay had picked up a small, fist-sized stone from the ground, set himself like he was throwing to the best batter in the high school league, then threw the stone as high and hard as he could. The stone's trajectory would have carried it to the other side of the clearing, if it had traveled that far. A few feet away, the stone hit something. There was the sound of glass breaking and falling to the ground. Now, a square piece of brown wood siding hung by itself about ten feet above the ground. It was strangely surreal, in that woods and clearing were all around it.

"You have *got* to be kidding!" said Jackson.

"Mirrors and well-painted glass about door-high all around the house. It gives you the appearance that nothing is here by reflecting back what you already see," explained Clay. He put his arm around Joni. "It's all yours, Mr. Jackson."

"Come out here, witch!" Jackson yelled. "We got business, you and me!" He bent down, grabbed a rock, and stood back up. "I'll break every piece of mirror on that place, witch! Come out!" Jackson threw the rock as hard as he could – not as hard as Clay, but quite respectably. Another piece of mirror shattered about eight feet above the ground. "I got plenty of rocks, witch, and people are dying because of you! Come out *NOW!*" he roared. He threw another rock, and another piece of mirror broke into pieces.

"All right, old man! I'm here! Now stop breakin' my house!"

The speaker was an old, hunchbacked woman. Her hair was sparse, gray, and tied into a bun on the back of her head. It had been years since she lost her last tooth, and her face had a wrinkled, pinched look. Her nose had been broken at one time, and leaned permanently to her right side. She walked with an ornately carved wooden cane, and took short, careful steps. The glasses on her face could properly be called "spectacles", because they were thick, and magnified the woman's eyes tenfold, so that she resembled a grounded owl. She wore an ankle length yellow skirt, sneakers, and a clean, but worn, red pullover sweater. A portion of the mirrored forest had opened as she came out, and allowed a quick glimpse inside the house, but not enough of a glimpse for details, because she shut the door behind her.

The woman stopped about ten feet away from the old man, and raised her cane in the air, as if it were a barrier between them. "What biz-ness do I have with you now, Ricky Jackson?" she said sternly.

Jackson pointed his finger at the woman. "That spell you gave me was wrong!"

"Did you ask for a summoning spell, Jackson?"

"I did."

"Did you get a summoning spell?"

"I did. But it didn't summon my sweet Gina!"

"Did you ask for a spell to summon Gina?"

Jackson shook his head. "You know I didn't."

"Then I gave you what you asked for."

"I didn't ask for a spell that opened a passageway to Hell!"

The woman shook her head. "That is not my concern."

"Excuse me. Ma'am?" interrupted Joni.

"What is it, little girl?"

"It's about to become your problem," said Joni quietly, as she pointed through the trees.

The Hellhound was running through the trees. Its neck was extended out as it ran, and its wings were tucked back along its sides. It ran quickly, and would be on them within a couple of minutes.

"A *Hellhound?* You brought a Hellhound down on me?" shouted the old woman.

"It's here, ma'am, and it killed our best friend," Clay shouted back. "It killed at least one cop in town, if not more, and *it's all your fault!* If you had given Mr. Jackson the spell he wanted, the doorway to Hell would never have been opened, and our friend would still be alive!" He took Joni's hand and ran toward the patch of "forest" that the old woman had used to leave the house. "So, if it's sympathy you want from us, you can forget it!"

She pointed her cane at Jackson. "You."

"Me? What about me?" asked Jackson.

"It was supposed to kill you. Then the door would have closed by itself," she said.

"Margo, do you still carry that? After all these years, are you still jealous that I chose Gina instead of you?" asked Jackson.

Margo? So, the witch and Mr. Jackson know each other! thought Joni.

"I *loved* you, Ricky! I could have made you happy!"

"I told you then, Margo. I said, 'I've given up on this love getting stronger.' I tried to be honest with you! But that wasn't good enough, was it? Now, you've brought *that*," he pointed toward the Hellhound, "and you need to *fix it!*"

A look of surprise crossed the old woman's face. She turned quickly to look at the Hellhound. It was almost to the clearing. The woman raised her cane, closed her eyes, and muttered something indecipherable. There was a flash from the cane that travelled the length of the clearing, then the light flashed again. The Hellhound slammed into something and fell back, dazed.

"There," said the woman. "I put a protective shield around the clearing. It'll keep it out for a little while...but it'll get through eventually. Let's go inside."

The woman led the way inside the camouflaged house.

The mist in Jackson's basement had completely hidden the floor. Terry's body was still at the bottom of the stairs, although it was now completely covered by the green glowing mist.

From the pentagram, a large tentacle eased its way along the basement floor. Its tip brushed against Terry's foot. It returned to the foot, and began further exploring the body. Finally, the tentacle wrapped around Terry's leg, and quickly snapped it through the doorway in the floor.

Unspeakable sounds, howls, and even maniacal laughter came from the doorway.

As if word were circulating that a door was open. An open door is an invitation.

And many of Hell's residents were accepting the invitation with enthusiasm.

The old woman led the trio into her kitchen. It had a homey, almost pleasant feel, with a fireplace against one wall. The fireplace actually had a black cauldron hanging over it, with water boiling. Joni leaned in for a closer look, and saw shirts and other garments. No witches' brew - the old woman was doing her laundry in the pot!

The sink had a hand pump, and was lit by natural sunlight filtering through the windows. The mirrors on the outside were two-way, and the old woman had been observing them all along.

The old woman gestured with her cane toward the kitchen table, and the four chairs surrounding it. "Since you're here, might as well make yourselves t'home. I'll put the kettle on for tea."

As the trio sat at the table, Joni finally broke down and started crying quietly to herself. Clay reached for her, and pulled her to his chest. After a moment, Jackson awkwardly offered Joni his surprisingly clean handkerchief as he patted her shoulder.

Margo the witch glanced at the crying high school girl. Her features softened a bit as she realized that Joni was crying real tears for her friend. They softened even more when she saw the awkward display of affection Jackson had shown for the child. "Ah, girl...I'm really sorry that your friend was killed." She took a deep breath. "And, Ricky, I'm sorry I tried to get you killed."

Jackson started to say something angry, but stopped, and closed his mouth with a snap. Margo was apologizing for real. Hesitantly, he said, "Apology accepted, Margo." He looked down at Clay and Joni. "Won't bring Terry back, but I...accept your apology." He glanced at Margo. "Now, what are we going to do about that Hellhound?"

"Hellhound will keep for another hour or two. Right now, we gotta close that damn doorway in your basement."

"Why, ma'am?" asked Clay.

"Now that they know the Hellhound is on the loose, the longer you leave that door to Hell open, the more that will come through."

Clay's face drained of color.

Jackson glared at Margo skeptically. "Now just how do you plan to get back to my house to close the damn thing?"

"Don't need to. We can close it from here." Margo lifted a huge book from a drawer in her china cabinet and plopped it down on the table. She opened the book and began flipping pages, until she found the page that she wanted. She lifted her cane, and began chanting the words to the spell.

The language was gibberish as far as the two kids and Jackson were concerned. They didn't understand them, and didn't need to.

Margo chanted for a couple of minutes, and, at the end, another bolt of light came from her cane. The light passed harmlessly through the door and was gone.

"Margo, what was that?" asked Jackson.

"The spell to close the doorway," Margo replied.

The mist in Jackson's basement swirled with eddies and currents. Unseen breezes from the pentagram rustled the newspapers in Jackson's recycling bin, and helped stir the mist along the floor.

No noise came from the area of the pentagram. All that had chosen to cross the threshold had done so, and none were in waiting.

When the light sent by Margo the witch arrived, it came through the front door, through the house, and down the basement stairs. It hit the pentagram, circled and covered it, and glowed so brightly with blue light that, for a moment, was brighter than the sunlight on that Saturday afternoon. The door's power had gained in strength, and when the blue light conquered it, and closed it, the two powers dissipated with a huge explosion. The explosion leveled Jackson's house, and the remnants caught on fire.

Ten minutes later, when the first fire trucks arrived on the scene, the remaining portions of the house were burned down to the basement. All the firefighters could do was spray water on the remains.

What was left of the chalk pentagram was washed away by the water and soot.

"That's great, ma'am," said Joni. "But how do we get rid of the Hellhound?"

Margo cackled. "Why, girl, that's easy! We kill it!"

"How?" asked Clay. "I saw the Perry city cops emptying their guns into that thing, and it didn't even faze it!"

"Don't be silly, boy," said Margo. "You can't kill a Hellhound with mortal weapons...unless they've been blessed! And blessed by a virgin, of course."

Clay and Joni looked puzzled.

Shaking her head, Margo opened a cabinet and took out a small vial of liquid. She shook it at Joni.

"See this, girl? It's holy water, blessed by Father Michael himself. You aren't the only one that slips into church now and again." She moved her attention to Clay. "Now, boy, I saw how you threw that rock at my house. Just like a baseball pitcher. Think you could do it again, and hit something small, while the pressure's on you?"

Clay looked skeptical. "Maybe. What do you want me to hit?"

Margo's brow wrinkled into a fierce look, and she leaned in closer to the high school senior. "You'll have to hit that Hellhound right between the eyes with a rock blessed with holy water. It's the only vulnerable spot that thing has! And you'll only get one chance!"

Jackson roared. "*You don't have the right to ask that boy to do that!*"

Margo whirled on Jackson. "You old bastard! Who else is gonna do it? You? Me? Her?" She pointed at Joni. "None of us have enough strength to throw it hard enough, and none of us have the accuracy to hit that spot! Except the boy!" She moved closer to Jackson. "And don't forget...*you* brought that thing down on all of us by wantin' to bring back the dead! So, sit back, Ricky Jackson, and let us pull your chestnuts out of the fire!"

"Clay, you aren't doing this," said Joni simply.

"If he doesn't, the hound will kill us all," said Margo.

"How hard can it be, Joni?" Clay said. "The thing is behind Ms. Margo's shield. I can easily hit it!"

"Ummmm...it can't be behind the shield I've created. The same magic that keeps the Hellhound *out* also keeps us *in*," said Margo. "Your rock would bounce off of the shield."

"*Woman...*" started Jackson warningly.

"Wait!" said Clay, holding his hand up. All eyes turned to him. "So, you're saying that the thing will be coming at me, and that I'll have time for one, maybe two, tosses of the rock? And I have to hit it directly between the eyes to kill it? And, if I miss, it will kill me, and then, kill the rest of you?"

The old witch nodded.

Clay said, "Piece o' cake."

"*WHAT?*" screamed Joni. "Clay, are you crazy? I don't want to lose you! Look at what happened to T-T-Ter-Terry...!" She collapsed into deep sobbing, with her head against his chest.

"Joni. Joni," said Clay, putting his hand under her chin and gently lifting her head to look into her eyes. "I can do this. It's a walk in the park!" He smiled at her. "Remember? Terry said that I should have gone out for baseball...that I would have been a great pitcher. I can *do* this!"

Joni looked into Clay's eyes. "You'd be a good pitcher, Clay. But this is too much. You're dead, just like Terry." She moved to a corner of the kitchen, crying.

Jackson patted Clay on the back. "You sure you want to do this, son?"

"Not like we have a lot of choices right now, is it?" said Clay dejectedly.

Margo came up with two good-sized stones, and the vial of holy water. "I need a virgin to put a few drops the holy water on these."

"Joni?" asked Clay.

"You can do it yourself, boy...Doesn't have to be a *girl* virgin."

Clay turned beet red, and took the water and stones. He fumbled with the vial for a moment, then got it open. As he sprinkled the stones, they began to glow with a blue light. Eyes wide with wonder, Clay turned to Margo.

"I'm ready, ma'am, but I have a question."

"What's that, boy?"

"What's your whole name? I've only heard your first name."

Margo looked surprised, then amused. She began laughing, and it actually sounded like a cackle!

"Boy, my full name is Margo Sardis! This county was named after my people!"

Clay nodded. "Thank you, Ms. Sardis. I appreciate it."

Margo sobered, then pointed at the boy with her cane. "Now, here's how it's gonna happen, boy! I'm going outside with ya, but just to undo the shield. I'll stay out with ya, but I'm no hero...if that thing gets too close, I'm duckin' back in here, and I hope you're right there with me!"

"Okay, ma'am. Let's go."

Joni turned. "Wait!" She ran to Clay, threw her arms around him, and kissed him like she'd never see him again. When the kiss ended, she looked into his eyes and said, "I love you, Clay Bowman. You'd better come back safe!"

"I love you, too, Joni. Don't worry, it's gonna be fine!"

"Come on, boy, the day is wasting!" said Margo.

"Good luck, Clay," said Jackson, and held out his hand to shake.

Clay shook hands with the old man. "Thank you, Mr. Jackson."

Clay and Margo opened the door, and went outside. Margo raised her cane and looked at Clay, who was casually tossing the glowing stone up and down in his hand.

"Are you ready, boy?" she asked.

"Ready as I'll ever be," Clay replied.

Margo nodded acknowledgement...or approval. Clay couldn't tell. Margo remained on her doorstep. Clay took a few steps into the yard. Margo raised her cane, closed her eyes, and began murmuring something indecipherable again. Clay spotted the hound about sixty yards away, and got ready to wind up. The blue light flew once more from Margo's cane, then the shield surrounding the clearing flashed blue as well. The Hellhound began bounding toward the pair as soon as the shield collapsed. Clay wound up, and threw the first stone as hard as he could toward his mark.

Clay missed. The hound had turned its head at the last second. It was moving fast, and had covered thirty yards already. Clay was stunned that he'd missed, but quickly wound up again. Margo held her cane aloft again and started muttering. The hound was at fifteen yards. Clay let the stone fly, and a bolt of blue energy engulfed the stone as it flew. The hound was at twenty feet when Clay threw the stone. The hound leaped into the air, planning to pounce down on Clay.

The stone turned in midair, going up to meet the hound. The stone found its mark, and hit the Hellhound directly between the eyes. The hound's leap was accurate, too, and it hit Clay. Both rolled a few feet, and both lay still.

Joni threw the door open, and ran to Clay's side, screaming his name. "Clay! Clay!" When she got to him, she threw herself to her knees and began shaking his shoulders, saying his name over and over.

Jackson came outside, too, and stood beside Margo.

"Do we have a truce now, old woman?" asked Jackson. "I mean, do you realize that I loved Gina with all my heart?"

Margo was quiet for a moment, then nodded as she released a huge sigh. "I understand, Ricky. I just have a problem letting go."

Jackson put his arm around her. "I'll be glad to be your friend, Margo."

Margo looked at him and smiled. "And I'll be content to be yours, Ricky. Oh! You're gonna need this!" She handed him some written instructions. "It'll take you to a few gold coins that you can change into cash. Your house is probably gone. Spells that strong, going against a doorway to Hell..." She shrugged. "They often close...violently, should we say?"

Before Jackson could respond, Clay opened his eyes and saw Joni hovering over him. "We've either died and are in Heaven, or I hit that Hellhound where it counted."

Joni started laughing through her tears, and began kissing and hugging Clay.

Margo had a couple of gallons of gas in a can in her basement. The trio gratefully accepted the gas, and bid their goodbyes and thanks to her, and hiked back to the car.

The Hellhound had glowed green, turned to mist, and disappeared.

To their surprise, Clay's car was in perfect condition.

"Margo. Had to be," said Jackson. "She did you right, boy."

Clay put the gas into the car, which started right up. The sun had just set on this Saturday, and they drove slowly back into town. As they passed the Perry Police Department, they saw that several sawhorse barriers had been erected, along with yellow tape that said, "Crime Scene Do Not Cross" over and over. Several patrol officers were manning the line.

Clay rolled his window down, and asked one of the patrol officers what had happened.

"Some zoo animal escaped, and a couple of officers were killed. But, don't worry, folks...it's been recaptured, and everything is under control."

As they drove on, Jackson said, "Can they really believe that it was only a zoo animal?"

"And that it was recaptured?" added Joni.

They drove on to Jackson's house. A car with red flashing lights on top was still parked at the curb. The car belonged to the Perry Fire Department. Clay parked behind it.

The house was gone. Only the basement hole and some foundation remained. As they got out of the car, a man in a fireman's hardhat that had just came from the basement waved and shouted at them, "Hey, you can't come up here! It's dangerous!"

"What happened to my house?" asked Jackson incredulously.

"Oh, are you Mr. Ricky Jackson?" asked the man in the firehat.

Jackson nodded.

"Sir, I'm so sorry. It looks like the gas main blew. Did you live alone, sir?"

Jackson nodded again, and braced himself for questions about Terry's body...but theydidn't come.

"Wow. We have been searching for you in what was left of the house, sir. I'm grateful that you're all right." The man made a couple of notes on his clipboard then handed Jackson a card. "If your insurance company has any questions, Mr. Jackson, my name is Ricky Griffis. I'm the Perry Fire Inspector. Just have them call me." He turned away, then turned back. "Oh, and we found a car belonging to an apparent runaway parked in your driveway, but we don't think he had anything to do with what happened."

"Thank you," said Jackson quietly, as he thought *That's what YOU think, buddy.*

"Good night, sir, and again, I'm sorry." Griffis left.

Looking over the house, Clay said, "Oh, my gosh. What happened to Terry?"

"We know he didn't get up and walk away," added Joni.

Jackson shook his head. "We may never know, kids. All we can do is grieve."

Clay shuffled his feet in the harsh light from the streetlamp. "Mr. Jackson, we need to get home. Will you be okay?"

Jackson waved them away. "Go on, I'll be fine. My car is in the garage out back. Get out of here."

Clay turned toward the car, and Joni leaned up and kissed Jackson on the cheek. "Take care, Mr. Jackson."

Clay called, "Call us if you need anything, sir." He and Joni got into the car and drove away.

Jackson walked toward the back yard and the garage, very aware that the trees surrounding his property seemed to isolate him. He looked up at the trees, and noticed a couple of green glowing things about twelve feet above him. He stopped, and peered at them in the darkness.

They look almost like the Hellhound's eyes...

A lighter shadow separated itself from the trees and stepped forward. In the dim light in the back yard, the shadow coalesced into a being. It was approximately fifteen feet tall, not twelve, had horns, arms as big around as Terry's body had been, and claws were at the ends of its fingers. Its ears were pointed, and, when it smiled, its teeth were many, and looked needle sharp. Its eyes glowed with the same green fire as the Hellhound's.

"PARDON MEEEE," the demon said in a deep, booming, gravelly voice. Jackson involuntarily soiled himself. "HAVE YOU SEEN MY HOUND?" it said loudly, and fiercely, as it reached its hand toward Jackson.

About The Author: T. M. Bilderback is a former radio announcer with a number of story ideas running around inside his head, most based on, or inspired by, classic songs. The author currently resides in Tennessee, and is writing feverishly in order to banish these stories from his head and into book form, before they drive him screaming into the street.

Other works by T. M. Bilderback
Nicholas Turner
If You Could Read My Mind
Justice Security
Mama Told Me Not To Come
Someone Saved My Life Tonight
Jackie Blue
Wake Me Up Before You Go-Go
Saturday In The Park
MacArthur Park
The Little Drummer Boy
The Night Chicago Died
Jim Dandy
Cow Patty
Hell's Bells
Black Dog
Lido Shuffle
Tales Of Sardis County
Don't Come Around Here No More
Junior's Farm
The Devil's In The Details
I'm Your Boogie Man
Colonel Abernathy's Tales
The Lion Sleeps Tonight
Heart Of Glass
Other Stories
The Wreck Of The Edmund Fitzgerald
Gold
Hot Child In The City
Eli's Coming
Other Novels
Empty Eyes
Story Collections
Greatest Hits

www.ingramcontent.com/pod-product-compliance
Lightning Source LLC
Chambersburg PA
CBHW020657180626
46816CB00003B/1334